Her Perfect Scoundrel

The Worthington Legacy
Book One

Marie Higgins

Text by Marie Higgins
Cover by Kim Killion Designs

Dragonblade Publishing, Inc. is an imprint of Kathryn Le Veque Novels, Inc.
P.O. Box 23
Moreno Valley, CA 92556
ceo@dragonbladepublishing.com

Produced in the United States of America

First Edition October 2023
Trade Paperback Edition

ARE YOU SIGNED UP FOR DRAGONBLADE'S BLOG?

You'll get the latest news and information on exclusive giveaways, exclusive excerpts, coming releases, sales, free books, cover reveals and more.

Check out our complete list of authors, too!

No spam, no junk. That's a promise!

Sign Up Here

www.dragonbladepublishing.com

Dearest Reader;

Thank you for your support of a small press. At Dragonblade Publishing, we strive to bring you the highest quality Historical Romance from some of the best authors in the business. Without your support, there is no 'us', so we sincerely hope you adore these stories and find some new favorite authors along the way.

Happy Reading!

CEO, Dragonblade Publishing

Additional Dragonblade books by Author Marie Higgins

The Worthington Legacy
Her Perfect Scoundrel (Book 1)
Her Dreamy Deceiver (Book 2)

Love's Addiction Series
A Wallflower to Love (Book 1)
A Governess to Protect (Book 2)
A Maiden to Remember (Book 3)

She is not the right woman for his brother, but is she the right one for him?

Lord Adrian Worthington wants to keep farthing-filcher women away from his older brother, but the tables turn when he finds Bridget Hartwell, a penniless country girl, vying for his brother's attention. For a man who isn't ready to marry, Adrian cannot stay away from the lovely lady whose kisses set him on fire.

As the eldest daughter of four, it is Bridget's responsibility to marry well. However, she wants to marry for love, which leaves the earl out of the running. Yet his younger brother is constantly on her mind—but falling in love with him is unacceptable.

Prologue

ADRIAN WORTHINGTON TAPPED his fingers on the table, contemplating the cards in his other hand. The noise at White's from the surrounding game tables didn't bother him, only because his mind was filled with more pressing matters. However, time was of the essence, so he must win this game.

He played Commerce well, he must admit, but he would never consider himself an addict like some of his chums. Adrian didn't mind taking their money at the gaming tables, and he enjoyed the feeling of victory when it happened. But he wasn't addicted to the sport.

All the men at the table this afternoon were related, and they all shared the same surname. Although Adrian enjoyed being with his cousins, when they crossed paths with an associate and the name *Worthington* was called out, Adrian and his cousins responded simultaneously. Quite often it was annoying.

"Adrian, are you going to play your hand or not?"

Adrian glanced across the table at Gavin Worthington, Viscount Lennox. The man's father was on his deathbed, and Gavin would soon become Duke of Englewood. For now, the man's only way to keep from thinking of his upcoming role was to gamble. Well, amongst other vices with the lovely ladies, of course.

"In due time," Adrian replied, pondering his cards.

"Perhaps your mind is occupied this afternoon, my good man. After all, your father just purchased a country estate for you and your brother." Malcolm Worthington produced a teasing grin as he glanced over the top of the cards in his hand. "I wonder what the true intention is behind the gesture. Does your father want to see which brother can stay alive the longest?"

Snickering circled the table. They all knew Adrian and his older brother, Collin, well enough to realize these were two men who had never seen eye to eye.

Adrian shook his head. "When you visit the estate tomorrow evening for the ball, you shall see that the manor is large enough that my brother and I won't cross paths often. In fact, we could stay apart for weeks if we plan it correctly."

Gavin raked his fingers through wavy, dark hair and shifted in his chair as he looked at Malcolm. "I'm sure you have it all wrong. Adrian's father is trying to end his sons' lives not by fisticuffs, but through marriage. I'm certain the marquess has planned that his sons will find genteel country women that will capture their hearts."

Adrian snorted a laugh and rolled his eyes. "How wrong you are, Viscount Lennox."

"Indeed?" Gavin arched an eyebrow. "Then tell me, why did he plan a ball for you and Collin and only invite the country folks?"

"Father also invited lords and ladies," Adrian quickly argued. "You did all receive an invitation, did you not?"

"Indeed, I did, but Collin informed me that not many ladies of nobility received invites." Gavin's eyes twinkled with mirth.

Adrian didn't appreciate the way the conversation had turned, making his stomach churn. His father wouldn't do *that*, would he? "Collin must have been heavy into his cups when you talked to him." Although he didn't agree with his older brother often, Adrian didn't believe Collin knew more about the ball.

The snickering bouncing around the table from Adrian's three cousins didn't sit well with him, making him very nervous.

He would prove them wrong. Even if his father had planned to have his sons marry country women, Adrian would change Collin's mind, because *he* certainly wouldn't marry a country woman. Those types of females were only after titled husbands, and Adrian would make certain they couldn't sink their claws into him or his brother.

"Are you going to play, Adrian?" Broderick Worthington snapped. "I'm scheduled to set sail next week, and I would like to finish this game before then."

Captain Broderick sailed to different countries in his trading business. Although the man was not titled, he was wealthy in his own right. Sometimes Adrian wished he had that kind of carefree life with no complications, free to sail across the ocean.

"Fine." Adrian placed two cards on the table and pushed them toward the dealer. "I'd like two more."

Looking at his new cards, he tried not to smile in confidence. He would win this round of Commerce. Sadly, winning money wouldn't give his mind any rest, especially not after hearing Gavin's opinion on why Adrian's father bought an estate for him and Collin to share. Was it a way to help the brothers repair their rocky relationship? Or was it because the controlling marquess wanted his sons to find destitute wives who were only after a titled husband?

Adrian couldn't believe his father would be so foolish as to hope his sons would fall in love with commoners, so it must be that the man wanted them to repair their brotherly relationship. He tried not to laugh out loud at the idiocy. The old man must not be right in his mind if he thought that. Regardless, Adrian wouldn't stay there for very long anyway. He would invest in stocks and find ways to build his own bank account.

When the game returned to Adrian, he grinned and placed his cards on the table, showing his cousins that he had won. Again.

Now, he had a party to oversee, and needed a plan to keep the commoners away from his and his brother's money.

Chapter One

"THIS IS THE very estate that will either give you happiness or bring ruination to your good name."

Adrian Worthington pulled his horse to a stop and shifted on the saddle, giving his cousin a quizzical stare. Trey Worthington hadn't been at yesterday's card game, so Adrian gave his cousin the grand tour of the estate. Trey had always been the humorous sort, and since the man married, his sense of humor had only expanded. At this moment, Adrian didn't know whether he should take him seriously or not.

"What the devil are you talking about?" Adrian yanked his leather gloves tighter on each hand. "Ruin my good name... Really. The idea is preposterous."

Trey tilted back his head and laughed heartily, which nearly caused his hat to fall to the moistened ground. In Adrian's opinion, that would serve him right. After all, his words were close to a hex, and Adrian wouldn't stand for it. *Ruin my good name... Indeed!*

Snapping upright, Trey grasped his hat to keep it from tumbling to the mud puddle next to him. He gestured toward the grand estate. Two separate wings adjoined the main house, and the land stretched on for miles. There was enough room for three different families to reside at Hanover Hall, but for the time being, only Adrian and his older brother would live there.

"Dear cousin," Trey said, "you are now away from the eagle eyes of your father. Who knows what mischief the two of you will get into?"

"You are wrong, Trey. Although Collin has returned from traveling abroad and is ready to plant his feet in one spot, I don't plan on staying here for more than a few years. Collin might want to live off our family's wealth, but I prefer to make my own money."

"Doing what, may I ask?" Trey rode next to Adrian's horse.

"Your friend, Dominic Lawrence, Marquees of Hawthorne, knows where I can invest, does he not?"

Trey barked with laughter. "Hawthorne? Oh, my dear cousin, you had better watch yourself. Dominic is very cunning."

"He is also a very wealthy man," Adrian quickly added.

"I suppose if you were to listen to anyone's advice, it would be to Hawthorne's. He is wise beyond his years. However, I can honestly say I've never known a bigger jokester."

Adrian wiped the moisture from his brow. England's mid-summer weather had plans to cook him this morning, even if it had rained during the night. If the temperature was this warm already, he wasn't looking forward to what it would be later today, especially with a house full of guests who had never met the Worthington family. He prayed they would not know about their wealth, either.

Inwardly, Adrian grumbled. This meant that every single woman in attendance—whether young or old—would be daydreaming about becoming the wife of one of the brothers. Adrian absolutely loathed fortune-hunting women. Most of the women he'd courted while living in Yorkshire were only after his family's money. None of them cared a whit about Adrian as a man. They didn't take the time to discover that he enjoyed taking long walks at sunset, or that he had started a collection of rare books, or that he wanted to find his own piece of land and breed horses. There was definitely profit in doing that.

The one woman he had *thought* different turned out to be just as unscrupulous as the others. He met her while visiting a school chum in North Devon. She was a very lovely woman, and at first, he thought she had the kindest heart. She led him to believe she didn't know who his family was, so he allowed himself to fall in love. He was ready to make an offer of marriage but didn't want to propose until he fetched the heirloom ring from his grandmother. Thankfully, before that could happen, he discovered she hadn't been honest with him. While away on business, she told everyone that she was going to be the next Lady Worthington, the sister-in-law to a wealthy earl.

Needless to say, Adrian had hardened his heart toward women who were only after snagging a rich husband, and he vowed not to let a woman worm her way into the Worthington family unless they were truly in love.

He mentally shook away the memory and focused on his cousin. "Trey? Are you and your wife planning to attend tonight's party?"

"Judith and I wouldn't miss it for the world." Trey grinned teasingly. "I'll be the one standing against the wall with a drink in my hand, watching you and Collin fight off all the maidens. I also plan on collecting bets to see who wins."

Groaning, Adrian rubbed his forehead. "I'm not looking forward to fighting off these country women. In fact, I don't want to attend the party at all for that reason alone."

Trey sat forward on his saddle, giving Adrian a stare. "Perhaps you need to let your guests know right away that you're not in the marriage market. In fact, if I have your permission, I shall walk amongst your guests holding a sign that reads, *Lord William Worthington is not for sale.*"

Adrian laughed boisterously. He wished to use *Adrian* as the name people knew him by instead of his given name of William. At least his family called him Adrian. "And you, my good man, would be the person who could pull it off. However, walking around with a sign might make me an outcast with our neighbors. If word ever got back to Father, he'd have heart palpitations and disown me."

Trey shrugged. "It was just a suggestion, but I understand about your father. It's best you keep your plans away from the old man, or he will find you a woman and write up the betrothal before the end of the week."

"You are correct." Adrian frowned. "Thankfully, Father won't be coming to the party, so at least I won't have to worry about tonight."

The other complications in Adrian's life could be put off, since there were now bigger issues at hand. If he had his way, he wouldn't even let their guests know he was a Worthington at all. Just thinking about warding off the overeager women seeking a husband exhausted him. And to think, the night hadn't even started.

Immediately, an idea popped into his head. The more he pondered the insanity of the situation, the more he liked it. Gradually, excitement filled his chest, making him anxious to try it.

"Actually, I have a better solution." Adrian laughed. "I shall have Collin introduce me as *Mr.* Adrian Worthington, his cousin. After all, if one's surname is Worthington, we are bound to be related somehow."

Trey snorted a laugh. "And I know Collin well. Your brother *will* make things difficult, if only to get you riled."

Adrian shrugged. "Then I suppose we'll have to keep him drinking port all evening. His mind will be spinning too much to think properly, and when he is that foxed, he doesn't talk much."

"Poor Collin." Trey gripped the reins and urged his horse forward. "There are so many ways I could play with his mind, you just cannot fathom."

"Indeed. I recall your pranks well, since I was the brunt of them many times." Adrian chuckled, keeping pace with his horse beside his cousin. "I'm certain I could imagine just what you could do to poor Collin."

"If I do something, I cannot let my beautiful Judith see. She would refuse to speak to me for a whole week, and I cannot have that."

Adrian knew his cousin enjoyed joking about Judith, but even a blind man could see how much Trey loved his wife and would do anything to please her.

"I only see one problem with your plan," Trey added.

"And what, pray tell, is that?"

"What if people ask Collin about the welfare of his brother? After all, the party is for both of you."

"I'll have Collin tell everyone that I had business elsewhere, and I'm not planning on residing at Hanover Hall for at least a fortnight."

Trey shook his head. "I wish you well with that adventure, but I don't see your brother agreeing to your prank."

"I'll make certain he goes along with my plan, even if I have to find something to blackmail him with in order to win this particular argument."

Adrian and Trey reached the estate at the same time and dismounted. After handing the reins to the waiting groomsman, Adrian led his cousin through the front double doors. The butler hurried toward them to take their hats.

The sweet aroma filling the house let Adrian know what kind of tarts and biscuits the kitchen staff were preparing for the party. The servants were already polishing the silver candlesticks and making everything in the spacious hall shiny and clean.

As Trey's gaze moved to the built-in bookcases made with dark wood lining the walls, Adrian studied the sunflower-cushioned settees to each side of the curving staircase. Father had done well with finding a country estate for his sons. Of course, the house wasn't as grand as the one Adrian and his brother had been raised in, but it would do for now.

"This is truly amazing," Trey whispered in awe. "I've never seen bookcases built into the walls such as these."

"My father told us that the designer of the manor loved working with wood, and as I take you throughout the place, you'll see just how much wood is actually used in each room. Father said he was also surprised how very little the owner was asking for this place."

"And are you certain the marquess won't be in attendance this evening?" Trey arched an eyebrow. "I'd think tonight's party would be the perfect place for him to boast about finding such a rare manor for his sons."

Adrian stood back and allowed his cousin to inspect everything at his leisure. Slowly, he moved toward the back of the corridor, leading Trey under the winding staircase and to one of the many doors that led into the kitchen. He had spent so much more time in a room similar to this one than his brother. Grace, their cook, had taught Adrian more about the important things in life than his tutor ever had.

His mouth stretched into a smile as he thought of all the late nights he had stayed up listening to Grace's tales of when she was a young woman traveling the world with her parents. Grace, God rest her soul, had experienced more adventures in her younger days than Adrian had at the age of twenty-eight.

From out the nearby window in the yard, a flash of teal caught his eye. The figure darted from one manicured shrub to the next. Scowling, Adrian moved closer to the window to get a better look. Then a second figure in pink hurried to join the first.

Finally finding a window that helped him see better, he studied the two women giggling behind a shrub. By the look of their faded dresses, tattered bonnets, and untidy hair, he suspected their purpose. The miscreants had probably heard about the party being thrown at the manor and were trying to glimpse the two wealthy bachelors who'd be hosting it.

Adrian gritted his teeth. It disgusted him to see women fall all over themselves in the hopes of being introduced to men of title and wealth. Their sole purpose was to entice men to fall in love with them just so they could haughtily stroll through town from one shop to the next, spending their husbands' money to their hearts' content.

He released a pent-up breath, trying to calm his ire. Adrian wanted to march out there and tell them to get off his land. He would not abide trespassers. Or gawkers.

As he stepped toward the door, his mind quickly halted his progression. He couldn't go outside looking like this, since he didn't want anyone to know he was the younger brother, William.

Grumbling, he swung around and looked for something else to wear. He rummaged through the drawers and the closets, searching for anything that wouldn't let these women know of his wealthy status. When he spotted a man's overcoat, still stained with dirt and green from the grass, hanging near the back door, he grinned. He would bet the coat belonged to the gardener.

In a flash, Adrian shrugged out of his deep coffee-colored riding frock coat, removed his cravat, and slid his arms through the gardener's coat. He brushed some of the dirt from the garment onto his trousers and boots. He even messed his hair a little and smeared some dirt on one of his cheeks.

As he opened the door, ready to reprimand the young women for being on the property, his words stopped in his throat. Another woman marched toward the young females, this one a few years older than the giggling geese by the bush. She wore a dress that wasn't as brightly colored, and her dark brown ringlets were tighter than the other two girls' hair. This woman didn't appear to be anything like the tittering half-wits by the shrubbery.

"Felicia, Jannette…" The woman in the beige dress stopped in front of the other two with her arms akimbo. "Pa is going to beat you alive if he hears of your exploits this time."

This time? Out of pure morbid curiosity, Adrian decided to hear more, so he quickly moved away from the door but kept it ajar as he continued to spy.

"But Bridget," the girl in pink whined, "we were curious about the two lords who've moved into the manor. We heard their family owns four more estates like this one. Can you imagine—"

"Felicia," the older woman interrupted, "you will stop spreading rumors this very instant. When you meet the earl and his brother tonight at the ball, that will be soon enough to know if what you've heard is correct." She scowled. "Unless, of course, Pa discovers what you've done and forbids you to attend—which, in my opinion, is what you both deserve."

Adrian rolled his eyes. His family didn't own four other estates like this one. Only three. But it disturbed him hearing that they were invited to this evening's event. Next time, he'd have someone who knew the people around town read over the guest list to make sure only *proper* and *disciplined* women were invited.

"Both of you know better than to go sneaking around on other people's lands," the brown-haired woman berated the others. "Ma would be turning in her grave if she knew what the two of you were doing."

The younger two women frowned, lowering their gazes to the ground.

The woman named Bridget pointed away from the manor. "Now hurry toward home before someone—"

When the woman stopped in mid-sentence, Adrian moved his gaze to her. Her attention was directly on him, and her surprised eyes blinked slowly. Apparently, he hadn't hidden himself well enough.

Her cheeks brightened and she took a hesitant step toward him. "Please forgive my sisters, sir."

Clearing his throat, he lifted his chin and proceeded out the door. The younger girls gasped and quickly scurried away. But the older sister stood stiffly, her gaze fixed on him.

"I apologize for my sisters trespassing on your lands. It shan't happen again."

"I would hope not," Adrian snapped. "That is very ill-mannered."

Her cheeks tinted pink as she scanned his attire. "Are you...

one of the earls?"

"I am not. The Earl of Hanover and his brother, Lord William, aren't currently at the manor."

Her eyes widened, and he realized they were a lovely blue. For a moment, he thought they resembled the sky on a clear day. He quickly pushed that sappy thought out of his head.

"Shouldn't the earl and his brother be getting ready for the party this evening?" she asked.

Adrian chuckled. "They will be ready, I assure you. We expect them to arrive very shortly."

"Oh." Her gaze slid over him. "Are you, um... one of the servants?"

"No. I'm their cousin from..." His mind scrambled to find a word. "Whitby."

She curtsied. "It's a pleasure to meet you. I'm Miss Bridget Hartwell. Our small farm is not more than two miles east of here."

"Will you be attending tonight's event?" Adrian asked.

"I suppose, since my father and my sisters were all invited." She sighed heavily. "That's assuming, of course, we are still invited after what my sisters have done. I must apologize again for their unseemly behavior. They should not have trespassed."

Adrian tried not to grin. This woman had read his thoughts. "I thank you for saying that." He bowed slightly. "I suppose I should leave now so I can ready myself for the party." He picked at the dirty jacket. "My cousin would be appalled if I showed up looking like this."

Her laugh was light. "Then I hope to see you later this evening."

"And I hope to see you as well, Miss Hartwell."

He watched her leave as he slowly made his way back inside the manor. Well, now that he had put his plan in motion, Collin couldn't possibly object. From here on out, Adrian would be the country cousin from Whitby.

Pausing at the door, he frowned. His brother *did* make it a habit of disagreeing with everything Adrian wanted to do. It would be interesting to see who would win tonight's argument.

Chapter Two

In Bridget Hartwell's world, there was no such thing as peace and quiet. Unless she left the house. Of course, being the eldest sister, there was bound to be some bickering back and forth, some tattling and some yelling, and a *large* amount of whining. Their mother had died ten years ago, leaving the raising of four daughters to their father. Sadly, most of the time Bridget felt more like a mother than a sibling.

The carriage bounced her in the seat as she stared out the window. Her father rode his horse next to the carriage as they made their way toward Hanover Hall. Sighing, she frowned. She envied her father, who didn't have to be in the cramped space with her two arguing sisters. And she wasn't looking forward to this ball as much as her sisters. Bridget did not do well mingling with high society.

Thankfully, her other sister Priscilla—who was a year younger than Bridget—was more mature than Jannette and Felicia. It was nice to have someone in her family who understood Bridget's dreams and disappointments, and who would remain her closest friend until they were old and gray.

As the carriage turned onto the path toward Hanover Hall, the three-level manor with two adjoining wings stood out majestically. Outdoor lanterns were placed along the walkway heading toward the manor, and bright lights from the windows of the lower-level rooms helped guide the guests to the front porch.

Nervously, Bridget wrung her hands in her lap. Not more than an hour ago, Pa had taken her aside and explained how necessary it was to secure a wealthy husband. The farm hadn't been producing as much, and the little funds they had been living off were quickly being depleted. Soon they would be penniless and living in squalor, unless a miracle happened.

Bridget believed in miracles, and she must do as her father instructed. She clenched her jaw. Being the eldest meant that she willingly took on the burden of finding the right man to wed for her family's sake, and she prayed everything would happen the way it should.

She glanced at Priscilla sitting next to her. In Bridget's opinion, Prissy should be the sister to land a wealthy husband. Her black, curly hair, bright blue eyes, and fair skin made her exceptionally pretty. Whereas Bridget could only describe herself in one word: drab. She had plain brown hair that was almost too curly for her ringlets to look natural, and the sprinkle of freckles across her nose proved how much she enjoyed being outdoors without a bonnet. She didn't even enjoy wearing brightly colored dresses.

The rhythm of the horse's hoofbeats decreased, and the two younger sisters gasped and practically hugged the window as they spied the manor while the driver prepared to stop.

Bridget's stomach twisted. Even though she loved dancing, the very idea that she was here tonight to find a husband ruined her mood.

She shivered and clutched her shawl tighter around her shoulders.

Priscilla glanced at her and frowned. "Are you not feeling well tonight? You have been awfully quiet."

Bridget put forth her best smile under the circumstances. "I've had much on my mind, but I'm well, I assure you."

The carriage stopped, and she waited for the driver to open the door. Inhaling deeply, she prepared herself for her role at tonight's ball. She would perform as a woman who was happy to be here. But if she could have her way, she'd wander outside after the first hour and find a thicket of trees in which to hide.

The driver opened the door and assisted Bridget out of the vehicle first. Priscilla followed, then came the giggling Felicia and Jannette. The younger sisters hooked their arms together and followed their father up the grand stone steps of the manor.

Father stopped and scowled at the pair, motioning with his hand for them to stop and wait for the elder sisters to proceed first. Bridget walked next to Prissy, but neither of them spoke another word to each other. Bridget was certain her sister was in awe of the place, just as she had been when she found her younger sisters sneaking around the grounds earlier today.

Embarrassment crept over Bridget as she recalled seeing the irritation written over that man's very judgmental face. Her mind stalled, trying to remember his name, but he hadn't given her one. All he'd said was that he was the earl's cousin.

Although he seemed irritated when she first started talking to him, by the end of their brief conversation, he had grown slightly more pleasant. He was a handsome man, too, which she found distracting—or was it his dirty clothes and messy hair that had distracted her? Regardless, she hoped to see him this evening, and perhaps she should beg him to make introductions to his cousin, the Earl of Hanover, Collin Worthington.

However, something in the back of her mind disturbed her about her chat with the earl's cousin. She found him very haughty for not having a title and living in the country. He had acted as if her sisters had trespassed on *his* land. Whatever it was, he was generally quite unpleasant to converse with, so perhaps it best that she *didn't* see him again.

Pushing aside her irritation with the Worthington cousin, Bridget stopped just inside the hall as a servant took her and her sisters' wraps. The mirror along one wall allowed her to glimpse her reflection. She had worn her fanciest gown. It was a grayish-blue, with a light peach sash and an overskirt of white lace. The white lace was also repeated on the bell-shaped sleeves. The heart-shaped bodice fit her snugly, just as it should, to emphasize her bosom. If not for her hair, Bridget would think she looked quite pretty. Maybe it was the sparkling lighting in the room that made her feel this way.

As Bridget and her family stood in line to meet the earl, rumors moved down the receiving line that the younger brother, Lord William, was not at the party. It mattered very little to her, only because it was one fewer man she needed to consider for a husband.

Bridget's father introduced himself to the earl then turned to introduce his eldest daughter. The earl was a handsome man, tall with broad shoulders, hair the color of wheat on a clear day, and hazel eyes. He smiled at her and bowed while she curtsied.

"It's a pleasure to meet you, my lord," she said sweetly.

The earl didn't speak much before turning to Bridget's sisters and giving them the same bland smile. Perhaps this was the only expression the man used during parties with strangers.

Her father had asked after Lord William's welfare, and the earl stated that his brother had business elsewhere that would keep him out of the area for approximately a month.

Father hooked his arm around Bridget's elbow and pulled her away from the crowd. He bent his head to her ear.

"Tonight, you must do everything you can to get the earl's attention. Is that understood?"

"Yes, Pa," she muttered meekly.

Her enthusiasm sank even lower. Why couldn't she just enjoy herself tonight like her sisters would be doing? Instead, she had to think of herself on a mission to catch the wealthiest husband. Truly, this wasn't fair—not to her, and especially not to the man. Then again, most titled lords were used to this. She wished there was a way to get out of doing such a dastardly deed, but alas, she must think of her family and not her own misery.

All the guests were people Bridget had met before, and it was good to chat with her close friends. But she did as her father requested and made certain she was within the earl's line of sight. Occasionally he glanced at her, but there was no indication that seeing her had caused a sudden love infatuation or, at the very least, given him a starry-eyed gaze of interest.

When the dancing began, the Earl of Hanover moved toward Lady Margaret, which was no surprise at all. Lady Margaret's family came from old money, and although the woman was nearly a spinster and not the most attractive woman at the party, she was still considered to be in the marriage market.

From across the room, Bridget's father threw her a scowl and motioned with his head toward the earl. She bunched her hands. What did he expect her to do? It wasn't as though she could throw herself in front of the earl, fall to her knees, and wrap her arms around his legs to keep him from dancing with Lady Margaret. That wasn't Bridget's way of catching a man's interest. However, she *could* imagine Felicia or Jannette doing something that ridiculous.

The brush of someone's fingers against her elbow snapped her attention to the person touching her. When her gaze met with the earl's cousin, she sucked in a quick breath. Although he didn't look as dignified as the earl, he was still rather handsome. More so now that he wore his evening attire and had cleaned himself up from their earlier meeting.

He smiled and bowed. "Miss Hartwell. How happy I am to see you have come." He glanced at Prissy, Felicia, and Jannette and arched an eyebrow before looking back to Bridget. "And you brought your two sisters… plus one more."

Bridget tried not to feel offended by the irritation in his voice. "But of course. Our whole family was invited."

She quickly glanced at her sisters, who were standing in a group with some of their friends, giggling louder than necessary. Bridget half expected the earl to watch the ladies who bothered him, but he didn't look away from her.

Meeting the cousin's eyes again, she forced a smile, feeling even more uncomfortable now. Although she didn't really want to converse with this condescending man, she would try to be nice. "I'm very… um, happy to see you are here, too."

He shrugged. "Where else would I be? I'm the earl's cousin who has been invited for an extended stay at the manor, and so I'm expected to be at these boring events."

She couldn't believe his rotten attitude. Earlier today he'd dressed like the gardener, yet now he acted as though *he* was the reason the earl arranged tonight's event. *Unbelievable!*

"Boring, you say?" she asked.

He nodded and leaned closer to her. "Didn't you know"—his voice lowered—"that it is my duty to weed out the social-climbing ladies who are not well suited for my cousin?"

She gasped as guilt seeped through her. Had he figured her out already? Was that why he had such a disdain-laced attitude? "Oh, please tell me you are jesting."

"On the contrary." He glanced over his shoulder toward the earl. "We all know the Earl of Hanover will be searching for a wife soon." His attention returned to her. "It's up to me, as his penniless cousin, to make certain the woman he chooses loves the earl for himself, not his title and lands."

Penniless cousin? It was difficult for Bridget to believe him when he acted as though he was the King of England, or at the very least, a prince. "Indeed? Is that the type of woman he really wants? One he can love?"

The cousin remained silent as he studied her face. Within seconds, his grin widened. It surprised her how just a genuine smile could change his whole expression. Dare she admit he was more handsome now? No, his holier-than-thou personality still made him ugly. She must remember that from here on out.

"Is that not what women like yourself want in a marriage?" he asked.

She arched an eyebrow. "Finding a man to love is certainly what I would search for. However, you must be aware how uncommon that is in most wealthy families."

"Yes, it's most uncommon, but not unheard of."

He folded his arms across his chest and rocked back and forth on his heels as his gaze moved around the room. Silence stretched between them, making Bridget very uncomfortable, only because she didn't want to say anything to bring back the conceited man. She rather liked the one with the sweet smile who didn't have rudeness spilling out of his mouth.

During the quiet minutes, she studied his handsome profile. A lock of his wavy, light brown hair had fallen across his forehead, but it was his startling hazel eyes that captured her attention. When he smiled, his eyes seemed to melt away her resistance to liking him. But she would not allow his smile or eyes to weaken her in any way.

From the corner of her eye, she noticed her father motioning with his hands toward the earl again. Inwardly, she groaned. It wasn't wise to forget about her true purpose here tonight. Getting closer to her target was important. As it was, too many people stood between her and the earl at this moment.

"Forgive me," she said as she turned away from her father, "but I just realized that you have yet to tell me your name."

When the earl's cousin's gaze met hers again, his eyes sparkled with mirth. "I cannot believe we have gone this long without proper introductions. I'm Adrian Collings, the country-bumpkin cousin that visits the earl from time to time."

Confusion filled her. Why did he make it a point to bring up his *impoverished* state, yet his actions were so very incongruous? Was he lying to her? Or was the strange man merely trying to play with her emotions? He must suspect she was only at this party to snag herself a titled, wealthy husband. If that were the case, she would have to thwart his mistrust quickly.

"Do you have a title I should address you by?" She turned slightly and slowly made her way toward the earl, trying not to look too suspicious.

He shook his head and walked with her. "I'm just a commoner."

"Oh, Mr. Worthington, although I've only just met you, I can see that you're far from being *common*."

"Indeed?" He cocked his head, watching her. "Pray tell, what is it about me that makes me stand out?"

"Well, earlier it was your dirt-smudged face." She chuckled.

His body shook with a silent laugh. "I must apologize for looking so sullied. If I had known there were three lovely visitors on our land—"

"But you didn't know," she quickly added. "And we weren't exactly visitors, since we were trespassing."

"So, what about now?" He arched an eyebrow. "What makes you think I'm far from common tonight?"

She took a quick peek at the earl. Although he was standing in line with Lady Margaret dancing the reel, his attention was diverted toward Bridget. Her heartbeat quickened. Why was the lord watching her and not his dance partner? Though with his narrowed eyes, he looked more mistrustful than dazzled by infatuation.

"Well, you see," she said, returning her focus to Adrian, "it is because you went out of your way to visit with me this evening." Knowing she was in the earl's direct line of sight, she stopped. Her father couldn't scold her for not having the earl's attention now. "After all," she continued, grinning at Mr. Worthington, "you have your pick of more than enough elegant ladies at tonight's ball, yet I'm the one you have chosen. And because of that, I'm wondering if you believe *me* to be one of these farthing-filching women you mentioned earlier, and you are trying to stop me from sinking my greedy claws into your cousin."

A sudden cough sprang from his throat, and his face reddened. Bridget grinned, knowing she had caught him off guard. But maybe that was the only way to keep him off her husband-hunting trail. She couldn't have him stopping her—or the earl—from wanting to get to know each other *if* they ever reached that point in the evening.

Once Adrian's coughing subsided, an all-knowing expression crossed his handsome face, making his eyes twinkle again. He linked his hands behind him, which made his chest appear wider than she first thought. Indeed, he was one fine man—country bumpkin or not. Yet if he really wasn't the penniless cousin, as she suspected, who was he?

"I must say, Miss Hartwell, that you're quite outspoken, and that not only surprises me, but it pleases me."

"Pray, did I say something out of turn, Mr. Worthington? I was merely pointing out the obvious."

"Obvious?"

She nodded. "Do you, or do you not, think I'm one of those deceitful women? Can you honestly say that you think I would lie to someone to mask my true purpose?"

Chapter Three

As Adrian stared at the lovely woman, his mind tried to figure out what she was really saying. She was playing with her words, for some reason. He was still very suspicious of her. He had been watching her and her family since their arrival, and from Mr. Hartwell's actions toward Bridget, Adrian knew what they were up to. Indeed, Miss Hartwell *was* a farthing filcher.

Now it was up to Adrian to keep her away from Collin, because for some reason, his older brother seemed to have his eyes on the lovely brunette, even while he entertained another woman. Adrian needed to keep them apart.

A servant walked by with a tray of champagne. Adrian stopped the man and took two glasses, handing one to Miss Hartwell and keeping the other.

He raised his glass slightly. "Here's to deceitful women and finding them before they can worm their way into the Worthington family."

She arched her perfectly shaped eyebrows. Her lovely heart-shaped lips twitched in a wicked smile. "Why do you think women are the only people who can deceive? Are you saying men cannot possibly be devious, as well?"

Adrian chuckled before drinking his champagne, keeping his gaze locked with hers. She slowly lifted the glass to her lips and sipped.

"Miss Hartwell, I must admit, you are a delight." He nodded.

Her smile stretched wider. "Mr. Worthington, I believe you are changing subjects to keep from giving me your answer." She stepped closer to him. "And that tells me you have secrets of your own."

"Is that a way of skirting around the fact that *you* have secrets as well?"

"Pray, what sort of secrets would I have?" She gave him an innocent look.

She twirled a lock of the curly ringlet that rested on her shoulder, pulling his attention to her gown. Although he had seen more elegant outfits, he couldn't stop admiring how well Bridget looked in this one. The light blue tones complemented her eyes perfectly, and the lacy sleeves barely hid her slender shoulders. For a moment, he wondered if her skin was as soft and creamy as it appeared.

He yanked his thoughts back to their conversation and stared into her pretty eyes. What kind of secrets did she have? He was sure he knew one of them, but were there more mysteries to this woman? Surprisingly enough, he wanted to find out more about her.

He sipped his champagne again before answering. "What if I were to tell you that I think you are after the earl for his title and lands?"

An uncomfortable laugh sprang from her throat, so she quickly took another drink of her champagne. Her eyes glittered like gems beneath the large chandelier hanging from the middle of the ceiling.

"Mr. Worthington," she said in a low voice, "you are a very suspicious man."

"One has to be if it is his duty to watch over his cousin and look out for his best interests."

She sighed, and her shoulders relaxed. "I am not foolish enough to believe a man of wealth will find me remotely attractive. However, I'm also a woman who should start looking for a husband unless I want to become a spinster."

Surprise washed over him. "Why wouldn't a man find you attractive?"

"Because a man of *wealth* would see the pathetic farm my family tries to keep productive, and he would wonder what I could possibly bring to the marriage."

Adrian cocked his head. "But you mentioned you were looking for love."

"Yes, but we also confirmed that love in a marriage amongst the titled is uncommon."

Chuckling softly, he shook his head. She was going to dance around his questions all evening. But that was fine with him. He found her refreshing, and he enjoyed their discussion.

"Pardon me for cutting in."

Collin's deep voice startled Adrian, and he whipped around toward his older brother. A foolish grin was pasted on the man's mouth as his gaze locked on Miss Hartwell. Inwardly, Adrian seethed. He couldn't allow his brother to fall under her spell.

"My lord." Bridget curtsied.

"Are you enjoying your evening?" Collin asked, stepping around Adrian and closer to Bridget.

"Of course. It's a lovely party." Her smile widened.

"I was wondering," Collin continued, "if you would honor me with the next dance."

Bridget's gasp was quite adorable, even Adrian had to admit. But really, did she not know that batting her lovely eyelashes and showing Collin her captivating smile *wouldn't* be an effective tool in her scheme?

Good grief, Adrian was having a hard time not letting it affect him.

"I… I would be honored, my lord." She handed Adrian her empty champagne glass as if he were nothing but a servant.

Collin held out his elbow, and she placed her hand on his arm as he escorted her to the dance floor.

Adrian clenched his teeth as he watched the pair dance.

Thankfully, it was another reel. But still, he didn't like the way Collin's eyes glimmered, or the way Bridget's demeanor had changed to one of shyness. *Shy?* Bridget was not shy. She was bold with her words, which Adrian liked. So, then why was she so different with Collin? It was as though she'd changed into a different woman entirely.

When another servant walked by with a tray, Adrian set the empty glasses on it and took a full glass. This time, he didn't sip it, but tossed it back quickly, as though he was a man who had been denied the luxury of a drink.

The longer he watched his brother and Bridget, the more his anger built up inside him. Why was this dance taking so long, anyway? But as Adrian studied her, he realized that the few times she had to hold Collin's hands, she hesitated.

Slowly, Adrian's tense body relaxed as he kept his curious stare on the woman. He still wondered about the shy way she looked at his brother, but why did she find it difficult to touch his hands? If this woman wanted to win Collin's favor, wouldn't she touch him more? Very odd, indeed.

When the dance was finished, Collin led Bridget back to Adrian. He still didn't approve of the stars in his brother's eyes when he thanked her for the dance.

Collin met his stare. "I need to talk to you for a moment… *cousin.*"

Adrian nodded and turned to Bridget's flushed face. "If you'll excuse me, I won't be more than a moment."

She smiled. "No need to hurry. I shall find my father." She curtsied, turned, and left.

Adrian threw a scowl at Collin. "What was *that* all about?"

Collin shook his head and leaned closer to Adrian's ear. "This game must stop. Too many people are asking why you aren't here."

"No, you're wrong, dear brother. I've heard the gossip moving around the room, and everyone believes I'm away on business, which is just as I had planned."

"William," Collin grumbled in a low voice. "You know I'm not happy with this game you're playing."

"But it's too late to stop." Adrian grinned victoriously. "Besides, I'm weeding out the women who only want you for your money. So, if you must validate my reasoning, I'm actually being an admirable brother by helping you find the perfect wife."

Collin scrubbed his hand over his chin and blew out a heavy breath. "William, you're confusing being admirable with being a nuisance, because we both know you've always been a thorn in my side. But unfortunately, we can't tell everyone who you are now. That will make us laughingstocks. And I won't have our family name ruined."

Adrian snorted, recalling Trey's warning earlier today. "My dear brother, when will you learn that people with money will never have their names ruined? Not only that, but our cousins attending tonight's events already know what part I'm playing. I informed them as they arrived. And stop calling me William. I'm Adrian."

Collin's eyes narrowed. "You need to grow up, and fast. Let's hope you can find someone who will lead you in the right direction, because heaven knows I cannot do it."

Collin turned to leave but came to a sudden stop as he glanced across the crowd. His eyes widened. Adrian tried to see what had disturbed his brother, but he couldn't find the culprit.

The older sibling swung back to Adrian and scowled. "I don't know how you're going to get out of this mess, but Aunt Beatrice just sashayed in as if she owned the manor."

Adrian held his breath. What was *she* doing here? But it was too late to start asking his brother why he'd invited her, of all people. The old windbag's middle name was *gossipmonger*. Their ancient aunt created rumors just to keep herself entertained.

Grumbling under his breath, he shook his head. How could he fix this mess? "Collin, I need you to distract her so that I can leave out one of the back doors."

Collin's glare darkened. "And once again, I'm covering up

your blunders. Mark my words, this will be the last time I do this for you."

Adrian rolled his eyes. "Indeed, you are a superb brother, and I should feel very fortunate for your assistance. But you're wasting time, so go stall that woman. Our *dear* aunt won't understand at all, and we don't need the countryside judging us for this cover-up."

"Judging *us*?" Collin's mouth tightened. "Take responsibility for your own mistakes, Adrian. I will not be blamed for this one." He turned and took long strides toward their nosey relative.

Adrian finally spotted the old windbag, and her weakling son shuffling beside her as if he needed his mother to do everything for him. The tall, frail woman's gray hair appeared blue tonight because of the lighting in the room. Aunt Beatrice leaned heavily on a cane, but she smiled brightly as she moved her gaze around, looking at all the guests.

It didn't take a genius to know what the woman was speculating. She would try her best to find her nephews a wife, and maybe, if she was lucky, she'd find her own son someone to marry as well. Nonetheless, Adrian had better leave before she noticed him.

Keeping his head lowered, he moved in between people, heading for one of the doors. Thankfully, he'd obviously played the part of the earl's cousin tonight well enough, because no one stopped his flight.

Placing his hand on the doorknob, he glanced over his shoulder toward his father's sister. He groaned. She was looking his way!

Raising her hand, she called out, "Lord William."

Adrian grumbled under his breath. He was certain that people would wonder why she said that name when William Worthington wasn't supposed to be at the party.

He rushed outside, breathing in the fresh air as he searched for a place to hide. The heat inside the ballroom was nearly unbearable, and at least out here he could think more clearly.

Aunt Beatrice would certainly come after him, especially now that they had exchanged glances. He hoped she and her son hadn't made plans to stay with them for very long. Adrian would definitely have to do something to shorten their visit. His aunt mustn't find out what he was up to, because if she knew, Adrian's father would hear about it soon. Good gossip traveled fast, even if his father was in Ireland.

Immediately, the image of another door popped into his head. Earlier today, he'd stepped outside from the kitchen when he first saw Bridget and her sisters. Aunt Beatrice wouldn't think to search for him in the kitchen. He doubted the wealthy woman—who didn't even know her servants' names—knew what that particular room was used for.

He hurried on, trying not to look as though he was running away. Several people had wandered outside and were in groups or couples. He didn't make eye contact with anyone as he moved around the house, heading for the back of the manor and toward the kitchen door. Finally, he reached a spot in the yard where there were no people, so he quickened his step.

Just as he turned the corner, he bumped into another person. In the shadows, all he could see was a woman in a light-colored dress falling backward. A squeak escaped her mouth as her arms flailed through the air.

He scrambled to grab her and, thankfully, was able to wrap both arms around her before she could hit the ground. She tightly grasped his arms. Teetering, he wondered for a moment if he would fall himself, but he quickly gained his footing and straightened, bringing her with him.

Finally, he was able to peer into the woman's face. *Bridget Hartwell?* Of all people, why did it have to be her that he bumped into… and was still holding as he gazed into her eyes? And why were her hands still clutching his arms as if she were afraid to let go?

"Oh," she said, breathless. "I'm so sorry for—"

"No, it's my fault entirely," he cut her off. "I shouldn't have been running."

Slowly, her body relaxed, and oddly enough, she didn't try to step out of his arms. And nor was he making any attempt to release her.

From a distance, he heard Aunt Beatrice calling for Lord William. Inwardly, he groaned. He couldn't let her find him. But more importantly, he could *not* let her find him with Bridget.

Chapter Four

BRIDGET WAS BREATHLESS, and it had nothing to do with almost being run over by a man in a hurry, or that she would have stained her best gown if she had fallen. But it did have something to do with the intimate hold Adrian Worthington currently had her in. Never had a man held her so closely, with his large hands braced against her back, as he stared into the depths of her eyes.

Swallowing the lump in her throat, she tried to bring moisture to her suddenly dry mouth. But it wasn't helping, as she was still in his arms. Her heart beat out of control, and she wondered why he hadn't released her.

Confusion flickered in his expression as he gradually relaxed his arms and pulled away. At least she could breathe better now. However, her body felt as if he'd taken the warmth from her. A chill passed through her, and she rubbed her arms.

"Mr. Worthington, what—"

"I hope you don't mind," he hastily interrupted while glancing behind him, "but I can't be here."

"What? I don't understand. You can't be… *where*?"

Grumbling, he grasped her hand. "Come with me into the kitchen."

Not waiting for her answer, he headed for the door where Bridget had first seen him earlier today. She stumbled to keep up with him, wondering what he was running from. He opened the door and gently ushered her inside, quickly following before he pulled the door closed. He leaned his ear against the wood, his breaths coming out fast and ragged.

She glanced around the kitchen. One lamp was on but turned down low. The air smelled like stew. They must have had beef for their evening meal.

"Um… Mr. Worthington?" she asked softly. "Why are we here?"

He growled and snapped away from the door, taking her hand once again.

"Someone is following me, and I'm trying to hide because I don't want to be found." His gaze jumped around the room, stopping on another door. "Come," he said, pulling her with him.

Bridget didn't dare argue, but she was very interested to know who was following him and, especially, why he wanted to hide. She had to admit it was rather intriguing, which was why she ignored the voice in her head telling her to stop him and demand answers. But there was another voice in her head—and this one shouted a warning, telling her that they were alone. That in itself could be very disastrous.

The door opened easily enough, but as they entered, she could tell right away it was the pantry. And it wasn't very large.

He closed the door behind him. Her back was pressed against some shelves, and he stood so very close in front of her. So close, in fact, that when she breathed deeply, the front of her gown brushed against his chest. Oh, this was not good at all. She couldn't see his face, but she could smell champagne on his breath.

"Mr. Worthington," she said softly, "can you kindly tell me what we are doing here? This is so very improper—"

"Shhh…" He placed a finger to her lips.

Her heartbeat accelerated. If they were caught… She shook the thought from her head. No, she couldn't get caught with him. For certain, her reputation would be ruined. Not only that, but the family would be ruined as well. Father would be disappointed in her for not trying her best to help the family. She must leave. Now!

"This is improper, and you know it," she muttered against his finger.

By the way his breaths blew against her face, she could tell his breathing had increased, too. Tenderly, he traced his finger along her mouth. The rustle of clothing was the only thing she heard as he shifted, and suddenly, his other hand slid around her waist, pulling her fully against him.

"Actually, Miss Hartwell," he whispered, "*this* is what I consider improper."

Before she had time to stop him, his mouth covered hers. She gasped and placed her hands on his shoulders to push him away, but the gentleness of his lips rubbing across hers stopped her. Tingles erupted in her chest and spread throughout her body. The longer his mouth was fused with hers, the more her body relaxed, until she couldn't feel the shelves holding her up. Instead, it was his arms and his body that kept her from melting to the floor.

Of their own accord, her hands wandered up to his neck, and she drew her fingers through his hair. A small moan rattled from his chest as he tightened his arms around her. Tilting his head, he deepened the kiss.

When his hot, velvety tongue caressed hers, explosions erupted inside her. Warmth merged with the tingles running crazily through her body. *Oh, heavens!* What was happening? And why did she like it so much that she didn't want to stop?

His kiss was so tender, so soft, yet so exciting that her mind spun out of control and made her feel as though she floated. What were the chances that he also felt this way? But she was just an innocent woman, and he… a scoundrel. Why else would he take such liberties with a woman he barely knew?

Finally, Adrian pulled away slightly, but left his forehead resting against hers. Both of them were breathing heavily, but at least her mind had started to clear. She should be angry at him, yet she wasn't. She should have stopped him the moment he took her into the kitchen, but her curiosity had clouded any thoughts of leaving. She should have realized her curious mind would win every time. However, it had never gotten her this type of situation before.

"Mr. Worthington—"

"I beg you… call me Adrian."

Her heart flipped. His voice was so deep and almost didn't sound like that of the man she'd been talking to earlier.

"Adrian," she sighed.

He moaned again and kissed down the side of her face. "I like how you say my name."

Excitement danced in her chest and her head continued to swim, but she couldn't let things get out of control again. If only she knew how to stop it.

"Adrian, will you please explain to me what just happened?"

His body shook with a silent laugh. "The earth moved. Could you not feel it, my sweet?"

He was trying to charm her, but she couldn't allow him to sway her thoughts. He was also still trying to seduce her, because his mouth touched her throat. As he continued to kiss the crook of her neck, a delightful shiver created havoc inside her. She clutched his arms, but mainly to hold herself upright.

"No, that's not… what I meant." She clenched her teeth, trying to hold back the sigh of pleasure threatening to spring forth. "What are we doing in here?"

"My dear Miss Hartwell." His arms tightened around her waist. "Have you never been kissed before?" He lifted his head and brushed his lips across hers. "Because I'm quite happy to volunteer as your instructor."

"Adrian…" She couldn't believe she sighed heavily again. "Please…"

"Please?" He kissed her on the mouth briefly. "Please… what? Are you asking me to teach you? I'm most certain you'll be a very responsive pupil."

A squeak escaped her as she imagined all that he would teach. But no, she must stay strong, or at least figure out how to become strong. At this very moment, she felt like a boulder sinking lower and lower into the dark abyss of the ocean.

"Please, tell me why we are… hiding."

"Well, I suppose," he continued, leaving light kisses on her lips, "we could do this in public, but I fear"—his kisses lingered slightly longer—"if we did that, we would make quite a spectacle, and people might start to gossip."

Why wasn't he understanding her? Or was he teasing her so he could continue kissing her? Although being close with him like this really wasn't horrid at all. It was the complete opposite.

"Adrian, I think you know what I mean."

He chuckled softly. "I do, but… this is so enjoyable. Don't you agree?"

She agreed wholeheartedly. However, she wasn't sure she wanted him to know that. "As enjoyable as you think this may be, I think we should stop." She couldn't stop herself from answering his kisses. It was as though something pulled her lips to his.

"Yes, we should," he whispered.

As she waited for him to stop, she continued to meet his slow and brief kisses. But soon, the mood shifted, and the kisses grew urgent. His hands moved over her back, stroking her, and bringing more excitement into her body. He tilted his head and deepened the kiss again. This time, she copied his actions, using her tongue in ways she had never thought possible. The passion between them climbed higher and higher. She threw her arms around his neck, not wanting this moment to end.

"William Worthington? Are you in here?" An older woman's voice rang through the empty kitchen.

Adrian's body stilled. Bridget hitched a breath. And just like that, their passionate mood was shattered.

Bridget was breathing so hard she could hardly catch her breath. His lips moved to her ear, and the warmth from his mouth made her shiver.

"Shhh..." he whispered. "She must not find us in here."

Who was the woman in the kitchen? Could she be the reason Adrian was in such a hurry to hide?

"William? Answer me. I know you came this way."

A few earth-trembling seconds crept by before the older lady's footsteps clicked on the kitchen floor, moving past the pantry, and she walked out of the kitchen further into the house.

Bridget didn't dare move, let alone speak. Thankfully, Adrian kept silent as well. She tried to listen if the other woman might still be in the kitchen, but all that could be heard were her own quick breaths blending with Adrian's.

Finally, he blew out a big breath as his body relaxed. "I wonder why she thought Lord William was in here?"

"Yes. Her actions were very curious, indeed."

He turned away from Bridget, and she rested against the shelves. Her heart still raced from the steamy kisses, but now that she could think more clearly, she berated herself for allowing them in the first place. She knew better than to kiss a man she barely knew, especially in a dark pantry.

Guilt filled her, and she wished this moment had never happened. How could she think back on this time and *not* consider herself any better than a strumpet? And if her father ever found out...

Tears stung her eyes. No! She couldn't let her parent know anything of the sort. She needed to walk out this pantry and the kitchen with her head held high and pray that nobody spotted her with Adrian. Also, she should never think of this moment again.

Slowly, Adrian opened the door and peeked into the kitchen. He motioned with his hand for her to follow, which she did on shaky legs. They tiptoed to the back door. He opened it and peeked outside and, once more, motioned for her to follow.

Once they were outside, he quietly closed the door and took her hand, leading her away from the manor toward the stables. The full moon gave enough light to see where they were headed, and they only stopped once they had rounded the corner of the stables, which blocked them from anyone's view.

Adrian let out a sigh of relief, bending over and resting his palms on his knees. A second later, he started laughing. Bridget scowled. What was wrong with this man, anyway? Had he lost his mind? How could he think that this was a humorous moment, especially when she felt like finding a deep hole and burying herself in it? Apparently, he didn't take this as seriously as she did. Then again, he was a scoundrel, and she was innocent.

She shook her head, correcting her thinking. She *had been* innocent, but no longer.

Straightening, Adrian met her stare. "Forgive me, Bridget, but the intensity of the moment had built up inside me, and I had to laugh in order to release it."

She folded her arms. It was difficult not to blame him for this mess, even though she hadn't tried to stop him. She wouldn't dwell on that now. Later, she would find the time to let guilt make her miserable.

"Mr. Worthington, will you now tell me what that was all about?"

His smile disappeared. "Why aren't you calling me Adrian, as I have asked?"

"Because I have realized the mistake in being so informal. However, now you must answer my question."

He raked his fingers through his hair. "That older woman you heard was Aunt Beatrice. She is slowly losing her mind. I don't believe she was really searching for Lord William, because she knows the man is away on business."

"Then why would she call his name at all?"

"I believe she was looking for me. She saw me leaving the party and tried to get my attention."

"And why did you not want to visit with your aunt?"

"That woman can talk one's ears off. She doesn't give anyone a chance to speak, and I didn't want to take the time to listen to her jabbering. She is very domineering and tries to control everyone around her. I pray she never becomes chummy with you, my sweet Bridget. She'll follow you around like a lost puppy, and she'll want to tell you what to do and how to live and, especially, how to act."

"That was why you were running and hiding?"

"The very reason, exactly."

Bridget tapped her fingers on her arm. "Now will you kindly explain why you felt the need to"—she swallowed hard—"kiss me?"

His humorous expression was replaced with one of desire as he moved closer to her. She held her breath, hoping he wasn't going to try to kiss her again. He couldn't even touch her, because she wasn't certain how her body would react. She feared that even his close presence would play havoc with her mind, even if her conscience told her Adrian Worthington was nothing but a scoundrel who used women for his own enjoyment.

"You see, my very passionate, sweet Bridget, when I touched my fingers to your lips to keep you quiet, and I felt your ragged, hot breath against my skin, I was caught up in my thoughts and wondered what it would feel like to kiss you." He stopped very close to her and drew the tips of his fingers across her mouth. "And I must say, I was not disappointed."

She was weak. He must know that. Why else would he keep trying to seduce her? However, she hated feeling guilty because of what they'd done, so she couldn't allow him to do it again.

With a trembling hand, she grasped his wrist, removing his hand from her mouth. "The kiss should have never happened, and I hope you don't think that I'm…" She licked her dry lips and cleared her throat. "That I'm *that* kind of woman, because I assure you, I'm not. I'm a true lady. Your kiss took me by surprise, and, well, I…"

"My sweet Bridget, please do not worry your pretty head about it." He cupped the side of her face. "I still respect you, and I know you're a true lady." He shrugged. "And if you want me to apologize for taking such liberties, then I shall. But I'll tell you now that I would be lying if I told you how sorry I was for doing that. If you must know, I'm very happy to have been able to kiss your luscious lips and experience your delectable passion."

"Yes, well…" She pushed his hand aside and moved past him. "We should not let that happen ever again. We were most fortunate that nobody caught us, and I don't want to take that chance again. With my luck, we would be caught, and I cannot have a sordid reputation." She swiped her palms down her gown. "In fact, I think we should both forget about tonight and keep our distance from each other."

He stared at her for the longest few seconds she had ever experienced. For a moment, he appeared to be saddened by her words. Her heart softened, but she didn't want him to see it in her eyes or hear it in her voice.

It was best that they were *never* alone. She would not allow this to happen again, especially since she felt like the fallen women her father had preached about in his Sunday sermons.

Finally, Adrian nodded. "Let's fix your hair before you return to the party."

She stood still and allowed him to stand close to her as his fingers plucked at her hair. Then he stroked her cheeks briefly.

"Bridget, my sweet, you might want to wait ten minutes or so before you return."

"Why?" she asked.

The corner of his mouth lifted in a half grin. "Because your lips are still swollen from our passionate kisses. Anyone who has been well kissed will know exactly what you have been doing during your absence from the ball."

She gasped, and her fingers flew to her mouth. Her lips didn't *feel* swollen, but she could still feel his mouth on hers. The butterflies fluttering inside her stomach reminded her that this was something she would never forget as long as she lived.

Chapter Five

ADRIAN SHOULD HAVE been very pleased with himself, since he could now tell Collin that Miss Hartwell wasn't the kind of woman to court—because she had fallen easily for a man's seduction. Yet he knew deep down inside that she wasn't *that* kind of a woman. Remarkably enough, the dejected pain in Adrian's heart told him that he had somehow allowed her kisses to affect him. The final blow last night at the ball was when she had told him that the kiss should never have happened and would never happen again.

It didn't take long for him to realize why she had said that. Because to her, Adrian was a penniless, country-bumpkin cousin of the earl, and not a wealthy man. There was no possible way she could have feelings for him. Not when Collin was still unattached.

Adrian leaned forward on his horse and pushed the animal faster as he rode through the countryside. Why had he thought Bridget was different? She wasn't. She was most certainly a farthing filcher, just as he'd suspected. She would never love Collin, especially since it appeared that she couldn't stand to touch him while they danced.

As he slowed the horse, Adrian's mind sped in a different direction. What had repulsed Miss Hartwell about touching his brother during the dance? Yet when Adrian was with Bridget inside the pantry, she had touched his arms, his chest, his neck, and even pushed her fingers through his hair. She had touched his hands a few times, but never once had she acted as if it repulsed her. And her kisses gave no indication that she didn't want his attention.

He pulled the horse to a stop and stared at the rolling hills in front of him. Over the years he had courted several women, and, of course, by now, he knew the difference between women who couldn't stand to be with him and women who desired him. Innocent Miss Bridget Hartwell was a woman who desired him, but apparently, she hadn't yet realized it herself. He might have to help that discovery move faster… without her knowing, of course.

A grin stretched across his face for the first time since this morning. Laughter bubbled up in his throat, and he couldn't hold back from releasing the sound.

"Oh, Miss Hartwell, you are in for a surprise." Feeling reassured, he urged the horse into a trot. "My sweet Bridget, I will help you realize that you enjoy the company of penniless men over men who have titles. I also promise to make certain that sure you cherish every minute of it."

In the distance ahead of him, another rider came his way. At first Adrian didn't recognize him, but soon he noticed the dark blond, wavy hair and the tall man with broad shoulders. Adrian stopped his horse and waited for his brother, preparing himself for the argument Collin would undoubtedly start.

"What are you doing out riding this early in the morning?" Adrian asked as his brother neared. "I would think the events of last evening would have kept you in your bedchambers until noon."

Collin scowled. "I would have still been asleep, but because you left the manor so early, and Aunt Beatrice saw you, she forced my valet to awaken me and fetch you back. She didn't get a chance to speak with you last night, and apparently, she cannot wait to have that chat."

Adrian tightened his grip on the reins. The old biddy had watched for him all evening long, and it appeared as though she wouldn't let the matter rest. Impatient woman. "When is she leaving? I pray it will be sometime today."

A nerve in Collin's cheek jumped. "Our dear aunt and her son, Walden, just arrived last night. It wouldn't be polite to ask them to leave so quickly. I thought they could stay with us for a fortnight."

"A fortnight?" Adrian asked in irritation. "We cannot have them visiting that long. Do you know how difficult it's going to be to have them around if I'm playing your cousin from Whitby?"

Collin arched an eyebrow accusingly. "And pray, whose fault is that?"

Adrian waved his hand dismissively. "Regardless of whose fault it is, she needs to leave posthaste, and take her milksop son with her. *You* need to make sure they leave today. She won't be very happy with me if I try to push her to go."

"That, my dear brother, is not my problem. It's *yours*, since you are the only one who wants them gone. I don't have time for your nonsense. I have people to visit today, starting with Miss Bridget Hartwell."

Adrian sucked in a quick breath. Panic mixed with anger filled him. Collin couldn't possibly be interested in a woman who found it difficult to touch him during their dance. "Are you jesting? Why not Lady Margaret?"

Collin's gaze narrowed. "Have you met her? Why would you think that woman would interest me?"

Adrian huffed. "Out of all the lovely ladies in attendance last night, why Miss Hartwell?"

A soft smile crossed Collin's face. "She's different from the other women, and I find her delightful."

"And you were able to get that impression of her during one dance?"

"Actually, we danced again later in the evening." Collin sighed. "She was more talkative then. And she is such a dear. She even kept Aunt Beatrice and Walden entertained for a few minutes while I fetched them some punch."

Adrian inwardly bristled. Because he'd needed to hide from their aunt last evening, he wasn't able to keep his eyes on Bridget after their interlude. "Well, I can assure you, Miss Hartwell is very outspoken. If you recall, I conversed with her for a little while."

"Actually, she wasn't outspoken at all. Perhaps she was that way with you because you irritated her so."

Muttering under his breath, Adrian clenched his jaw. "No, that is not it at all." He tried to calm the annoyance rising inside him. "But I can tell you that she is not your type. In fact, I think you should court Lady Margaret. From what I've heard, her family has money, so at least we know she isn't marrying you because of your wealth."

"Then *you* court her," Collin snapped.

Adrian snorted. "I'm not going to court anyone—not for a few years."

"Although I found Lady Margaret comely, I found Miss Hartwell lovelier. She was such a delight, and when she went out of her way to chat with Aunt Beatrice and Walden, that made me realize how special she is—so much more, in fact, than the other ladies I conversed with. So, I don't know why you cannot approve."

"She… she…" *Think, Worthington!* "Because she wouldn't make a very good countess."

Collin tapped a finger on his chin. "And what makes you come to that conclusion?"

Adrian scrambled to come up with something plausible. Telling his brother that the woman was in his arms in a dark pantry for more than twenty minutes wouldn't be a good idea. "Did you not see the freckles on her nose?" He shook his head. "She obviously doesn't approve of bonnets, and both of us know what society expects from ladies who gain a title."

"Freckles? Really, Adrian? You are being ridiculous, as always." Collin lifted his chin haughtily. "Besides, I found they gave her lovely face a glow of enchantment."

Adrian hated to admit that he found them adorable as well. And Bridget was certainly a beautiful woman with a fun sense of humor and a quirky personality. Not only that, she had the most kissable lips…

"And since I'm the one looking for a wife—not you," Collin continued, "I don't see why you are trying to convince me otherwise. You should be relieved I'm not trying to find *you* a wife, as well."

"I'll not allow you to waste your time," Adrian grumbled, hating that his brother was trying to control him. That was their father's duty, not Collin's. And even then, Adrian wouldn't allow his father to do such a dreadful thing.

"Stop trying to convince me that Miss Hartwell wouldn't make a fine countess. Whether you like it or not, I will call upon her this morning, and if I feel the same as I did last night, I'm going to ask her father's permission to court her."

Adrian scowled. "If you didn't want my opinion of the woman, why have you ridden all the way out here to tell me?"

Collin laughed. "I wanted to see your reaction, and now that I know how the woman irritates you, that tells me how much I'm going to enjoy her company." He nodded. "Good day, brother. I hope you find yourself in better spirits when you get home. After all, *you* are the one who has to convince Aunt Beatrice to leave."

As Collin turned his horse around and rode back toward the estate, Adrian mumbled curses under his breath. There was no way he could allow his brother to court Bridget. Not until he proved his theory of her being a calculating farthing filcher who was only after a title. He must discover if she could still be attracted to a penniless man before he would allow his brother to court her.

But now Adrian had to think of a way to keep her from seeing Collin this morning.

Suddenly, an idea popped into his head. Grinning, he kicked

his horse into a run, heading directly toward the Hartwell farm.

BRIDGET HUMMED A joyful tune as she hung the laundry in the backyard. She had been up since the crack of dawn, and a smile hadn't left her face since. Unfortunately, she didn't know what exactly it was about last night that made her smile. Was it Adrian's exciting kisses, or the fact that she had somehow gotten the Earl of Hanover's attention?

No, it couldn't have been Adrian's kiss. She had felt like such a wanton woman after leaving him at the stable, and she couldn't shake off the guilt. So, it must be Collin that kept her smiling.

"This is the last of the laundry." Pricilla set the basket on the ground of newly washed clothes. As she straightened, she pushed her wavy hair away from her forehead.

"Thank you, Prissy. I was almost ready for more." Bridget continued humming and lifted a wet garment up to the clothesline.

"Bridget, this really must stop."

She glanced at her sister. "What has to stop?"

"The humming. Either you tell me why you are so happy, or I'm going to have Pa call the physician and have you examined thoroughly."

Laughing, Bridget shook her head. "I'm fine, I assure you."

"Are you smiling because the earl danced with you twice last night?"

Bridget shrugged. "Could be, I suppose." Images of Adrian popped into her head, making her heart flip-flop and her lips tingle with awareness. *Stop it, Bridget!*

She quickly pushed her memories away. Perhaps seeing a doctor was a good idea after all. How else could she stop thinking about Adrian?

"Lord Hanover is a very sweet man," Priscilla said.

"Yes. He has a certain charm about him that I cannot stop thinking about."

Pricilla lifted one of Pa's shirts out of the basket of wet clothes. "He also danced with me."

Bridget held her breath, waiting for her elation to deflate, but it didn't. She felt the same now as she had a minute ago. For some reason, it didn't bother her that he had also danced with her sister. "I'm sure he danced with a lot of women last night."

"He did."

The sadness in Priscilla's voice caught Bridget's attention. She looked over the top of clothesline at her sister. "Were you hoping he would just dance with you?"

"Lord Hanover was the main attraction. I suppose if his brother were in attendance, there would have been two men to watch." Prissy laughed forcefully. "We all know and understand the rules of not dancing more than twice with the same lady, so why would I want him to go against society's boundaries?"

"Well, I'm glad." Bridget nodded. "Because not only would he have ruined the lady's reputation, but his name would have been dragged through the mire, as well."

"Yes, I'm aware of that."

Once again, Adrian's face popped into her mind—images of them in each other's arms with their mouths locked in a passionate kiss. Inwardly, she groaned. What they had done in the kitchen's pantry could have ruined her completely. She was very fortunate Aunt Beatrice hadn't found them, and that the evening's dark shadows had kept them from being noticed as they snuck out of the kitchen's back door.

Priscilla hung up the shirt, but didn't move from where she stood. "Bridget, do you think he's going to call on you today?"

Bridget's heartbeat accelerated slightly. *Oh, heavens!* Would Adrian be that bold? Why would he come to see her, anyway?

Her mind quickly jerked her back to the conversation she had with her sister before thoughts of Adrian had intruded. They were talking about the earl, *not* his cousin.

She breathed a little easier. "I couldn't say. We had a nice talk, and he introduced me to his aunt and her son. But that was the essence of our evening together. Besides the dance, that is."

"Pa is hoping the earl comes to call on you today."

Bridget released a heavy breath, remembering her father's thoughts. "Yes, I'm sure Pa is in his study with his Bible in hand, praying for the earl's visit right now."

There was silence for a few seconds before Priscilla chuckled. "When I was chatting with Charlotte last night at the ball, she mentioned how strange it was that such a prominent family as the Worthingtons would purchase that particular estate."

Bridget glanced at her sister. "And why is that?"

"Because it's not as grand as some of their other estates."

Bridget gave her sister a quizzical stare. "Do you have firsthand knowledge of that?"

Frowning, Prissy looked down at the ground. "No."

"Then there must be a good reason why the estate was purchased." Bridget hung up another garment. "After all, it is a fine piece of land, and the manor is quite impressive."

"And if good fortune is on our side," Prissy said in a hurry, "you'll be the mistress of Hanover Hall."

Bridget created a make-believe wedding in her mind, with her wearing a lovely gown and flowers decorating the church. Her father would officiate the ceremony, and all of her sisters would wear pretty gowns and stand close by, giving her support. The chapel would be full of people who were happy for her union with a titled man.

And the man who she'd take as her husband… wasn't Collin. In fact, the man in her dream had darker hair.

Recognizing the face of the man, Bridget belted out a laugh. What was she thinking? Adrian Worthington should *not* be in her dreams, or her thoughts.

"Mistress of Hanover Hall?" Bridget shook her head. "That will never happen, Prissy."

"You never know."

Priscilla smiled, but it wasn't full. She picked up another shirt and pinned it to the clothesline. A few minutes of silence passed. A small breeze wafted through the trees, making the leaves rustle, but that was the only noise. Bridget realized how much she hated the stillness, because it gave her mind access to dreams of things that would never come to pass, and things that should *never* have happened in the first place.

"Bridget? Didn't the earl tell Father that his brother was away on business?"

Bridget sighed, welcoming a different topic of conversation. "Yes, why do you ask?"

"Last night, I talked to friends who overheard the earl's aunt calling for Lord William. If the brother was gone, why would his aunt think he was in attendance?"

Bridget picked up another wet garment from the basket. "That's a very good question. When I stepped outside briefly during the evening, I also heard the old woman calling for Lord William. It was very strange, indeed."

"I thought you would know, since you spoke with her last night."

Bridget shrugged. "The woman didn't mention Lord William to me at all. She was more focused on telling me about wonderful Lord Hanover was and what a fine husband he would make."

Prissy giggled behind her hand. "Another rumor I heard was that his aunt mentioned seeing Lord William sneaking out of the ball with a woman on his arm."

Bridget sucked in a breath as her chest tightened. She opened her mind again, recalling when Adrian had taken her by the hand and pulled her into the kitchen, and then into the pantry. Later, Aunt Beatrice had entered the kitchen, calling for Lord William.

Adrian's voice entered her head. *She is slowly losing her mind. I don't believe she was really searching for Lord William, because she knows the man is away on business.*

Confusion filled Bridget as she scrambled to make sense of everything. Was it a coincidence that the aunt had supposedly seen Lord William leaving, yet Adrian had been the one leaving the party—with a woman?

Bridget chuckled lightly and shook her head. What was she thinking? Adrian definitely was *not* Lord William. He didn't even act like a titled man. He was certainly a scoundrel of the worst kind, one she should have never tangled with.

She breathed easier. It was difficult not to listen to gossip. "The poor woman must be delusional."

"Yes, that's what I thought, as well."

As Bridget proceeded to hang the rest of the garments, her thoughts wouldn't leave Adrian and everything that happened last night. He'd tried his hardest to make her aware that he wouldn't allow fortune-hunting women to catch his cousin. And then he whisked her off to the kitchen to kiss her passionately. Now she wondered if that was Adrian's way of keeping her from the earl.

Her heart sank. Adrian Worthington was such a scoundrel. He had kissed her because that was what men like him did when they found themselves alone with a woman. And he did it so that his cousin would never court her.

Suddenly, the happy feeling that had consumed her all morning disappeared, and emptiness filled her, along with a stronger burst of guilt. How could she have enjoyed being in his arms and kissing him as if they were the only two people at the party? He'd been very tender and sweet, but full of passion. Now she knew it was all an act.

The conversation about Lord William kept creeping into her thoughts. Adrian had tried to make her think that Aunt Beatrice had lost her mind, yet after meeting and visiting with the old woman, not once did Bridget think the woman wasn't in full control of her thoughts. Aunt Beatrice was quite intelligent, in fact.

Another thing that bothered Bridget was that not once did Collin go out of his way to introduce his cousin, Adrian Worthington, to any of the guests at the party. Aunt Beatrice didn't mention Adrian being in attendance, either. If he were a close relative, why hadn't his family acknowledged him?

The rumors had circulated about Lord William being at the ball, but nobody had met him. There was certainly a secret going on in the Worthington family, at least between the earl and Adrian… who, although they had different hair coloring, looked remarkably alike. Bridget had cousins, but she and her sisters didn't resemble them at all.

Could the secret the so-called cousins were keeping be that Adrian was the earl's brother?

A sharp pain gripped her heart as though a knife had been plunged into her chest, which made it difficult to breathe. How had she been so gullible? Why hadn't she seen through Adrian's deceit? Then again, he had left enough hints. He had told her that his main purpose at the ball was to keep farthing-filching women away from the earl.

Would a cousin really do something so personal, or would a brother?

Closing her eyes, she rubbed her throbbing forehead. She had been deceived, not only by Adrian, but Lord Hanover as well.

Her stomach churned, threatening to bring up her breakfast at any moment. Thankfully, most of her chores had been finished earlier this morning, because now she felt like lying down for the rest of the day, or for the next month. It didn't matter how long she slept, just that she could be secluded and not have to look at anyone, especially the two Worthington men she'd met last night.

"What is amiss, dear sister?" Priscilla's hand touched Bridget's arm. "Your face is so pale."

"I have a headache." She looked at Prissy. "It came on quickly, and now I feel the need to lie down."

"Yes, you should. I'll finish up here."

Walking sluggishly, Bridget made her way back toward the house. Shame ate away at her memories, making her feel lower than the sinners her father preached about during his Sunday sermons. Why had she been so free with her kisses with Adrian last night? She could have pushed him away several times. But like a lamb being led to slaughter, she'd allowed Adrian to take her in a private room and let him teach her about passionately kissing a man.

His words echoed in her mind. *I'm quite happy to volunteer as your instructor.*

Why couldn't she forget what happened? Why hadn't she ignored him and remembered that he had been rude when they first met? And if Adrian was really the earl's younger brother, William, it was no wonder he'd set out to seduce her. He wanted to keep her away from his brother.

Tears stung her eyes. Guilt was a heavy burden to carry, and she wanted to scream.

As she passed the chicken coop, the birds squawked louder than usual, and the noise made the pounding in her head worse. She glanced inside the coop, and a pair of men's riding boots caught her attention. She followed them up past the man's muscular legs, up over his riding jacket, and came to rest on a handsome face.

"Adrian," she gasped, moving inside the coop. "What in heaven's name are you doing?"

"Trying to hide."

Was this another ploy of his to get her away from his brother? But now he was at her home. Anger built up inside her, and she wanted to slap him. She wanted to yell at him for everything he had put her through. But first, she needed to know if he was truly Lord William. Somehow, she had to trick him to get his confession.

"Not again." She rolled her eyes. "Why are you always trying to hide? This isn't the pantry, you know."

"Shh…" He moved from the corner of the coop and came toward her. "Is there some place we can talk in private?"

"I don't think so, *Mr.* Worthington," she said, recalling that she was not going to call him by his given name again. "Our pantry isn't enclosed as the one in the manor's kitchen is."

His gaze narrowed on her as a frown touched his features. "Bridget, is something amiss?"

Her heart tugged with the betrayed emotion. Why did he act so caring when she knew otherwise? If he didn't leave now, she might just empty her stomach all over him—or cry. She didn't want to do either.

"Please leave, Mr. Worthington. I have a headache, and I'm going to lie down."

She turned, but he grasped her arm. "We really need to talk. I think my aunt knows about us."

Panic filled her, but then she suddenly recalled what her sister had said about Aunt Beatrice calling Lord William's name. She glared at Adrian. "I don't understand. How could your aunt possibly—"

"Shh..." He placed his hand on her mouth. "Please. It won't take very long. Where can we talk in private?"

She pushed his hand away. Their first kiss had happened after he touched her mouth. She couldn't let that happen again. "Well, we certainly cannot meet anywhere around my family's farm." She tried to make her mind work as she rubbed her throbbing temples. "There is a pond two miles east of here. We can meet there."

"I don't know this area very well."

She pointed toward the east. "Head in that direction and you'll run across it. I shall meet you there shortly."

He smiled. "Don't be long."

They carefully stepped out of the chicken coop. He hurried to his horse and mounted. She checked for her family's whereabouts to make sure they couldn't be observed. She couldn't possibly tell her pa what happened last night, which meant he should not catch sight of Adrian right now.

As soon as he was hidden by the trees, she hurried into the house to change her clothes. The dress she had on was one she wore when she did her chores. She didn't want to meet him smelling like sweat, hay, and laundry soap.

After changing into one of her day dresses, she brushed her hair. Just as she thought about winding it in a coil, she decided against it. What was she doing? Why was she trying to impress him when she would never forgive him for lying to her and making her feel this terrible? However, she would meet him at the pond—but she would tell him her feelings and make him promise to never speak to her again.

And no matter how hard he tried—because she suspected he would—she would *not* let him kiss her.

Chapter Six

ADRIAN PACED IN front of the pond as thoughts swirled in his head. *What am I doing?* He had originally started this disguise with the hope of getting to talk with some of the ladies Collin found interesting and to see if they were good enough for his brother. Yet Adrian just *had* to kiss one of them—and enjoy it—and now guilt overwhelmed him.

Every time he talked to Bridget, a lie would blurt out of his mouth. If roles were reversed, he would never forgive a woman if she deceived him in such a way. He wouldn't blame Bridget if she hated him.

But he couldn't tell her yet. There was still so much to talk about, and so many more kisses, before he could confess what he had done. He really wanted to get to know her better, even if it meant she would never forgive him once the truth was out. Indeed, he was the worst kind of rogue. And he deserved her wrath… just not yet.

What a mess he had made of his life already. Trey had been correct when he said that Hanover Hall would either bring Adrian happiness or bring him ruination. He felt that by the time everything was out in the open, nobody in polite society would want to talk to him.

Perhaps he had been too hasty deciding to play the part of a country bumpkin. And for what? Just because he didn't want mothers forcing introductions to their unwed daughters? Indeed, he was pathetic.

Adrian moved away from the pond that was surrounded by trees, and out into the clearing. Where was Bridget? He'd expected her to ride up on a horse to meet him minutes after he arrived, but a good fifteen minutes had passed and there was no sign of her. She couldn't have forgotten. Perhaps she had decided not to come at all.

Grumbling, he stomped back toward the pond. If he had to ride back to her farm and kidnap her just so she wouldn't visit with his brother, Adrian would do it. He couldn't have Collin falling in love with this particular Hartwell sister.

The pounding of horses' hooves jerked him out of his discouraging thoughts, and he darted back into the clearing. When he saw Bridget on the horse—riding astride, no less—and coming toward him, his heartbeat quickened. He felt anxious, waiting for her to stop the horse so that he could touch her while helping her down.

She stopped the animal, and Adrian reached up to help her dismount. Ignoring his help, she leaned forward as she swung one leg over to meet with the other, and hopped down without his assistance. Emptiness filled him as he dropped his arms to his sides. She avoided his gaze, and a pain of yearning tightened his chest, making him realize he needed to see her bright blue eyes again.

As he skimmed over her attire, he nearly lost his breath. She had been lovely last night, but now… she was alluring. She wore a plain burnt-peach day dress—different from the dress she was wearing when he saw her at the chicken coop—but it was the way her long hair hung down her back and flowed over her shoulders that caused his mind to stop and his heartbeat to accelerate.

And, of course, she wore no bonnet. He almost laughed to think she wasn't being proper, but he was too mesmerized by her beauty to do anything but stare. He was probably drooling, too.

He used his fingers to wipe his mouth, just in case.

"Thank you for meeting me," he told her.

She led the horse to the nearest tree, tying the reins to a limb. "We need to make this quick. If we take too long, my family will certainly ask questions that I don't want to answer."

Tenderly, he took her hand and walked toward the pond. The surrounding trees would help keep their talk a little private. But after two steps, she yanked her hand away and folded her arms.

Disappointment grew inside him, and he gritted his teeth. Why couldn't he stop his craving to touch her? It was obvious that she didn't want any kind of attention he was willing to pour upon her.

"I must say," he said, glancing at her, "I'm surprised your hair is not styled."

She shrugged. "I had planned on resting to get rid of my headache, so I didn't see a need to style it just to meet you."

The snappy tone of her voice worried him. She sounded upset, and that she just didn't care that they were together right now. He needed to change her mind. The tightness in his chest required it.

"I'm not saying that I don't approve of your hair." He glanced over it again. "I like it long and flowing over your shoulders. It fits your bold personality."

They stopped at the same time. Her throat constricted in what must have been a hard swallow as she stared at the water. The wind created small waves, which was mesmerizing in itself, but he would rather look at her.

Sighing, she dropped her arms to her sides. He immediately took hold of her hand, being as gentle as he would if holding a porcelain dish. She tried to pull away, but he wouldn't let her go. He couldn't. The urgency building inside him wouldn't allow it. Instead, he tugged her closer until he could slip his arm around her waist. Finally, her gaze jumped up and met his as she pressed her palms against his chest. It hurt that she wasn't smiling.

"Mr. Worthington, if you don't mind, I would rather not get personal like we were last evening."

He stroked her cheek. "But what if I *do* mind?"

One of her eyebrows lifted. "Then I suppose you shall have to quickly become accustomed to disappointment."

She tried to move out of his arms again, but he tightened his hold. "Bridget? What is bothering you? Why are you like this? The last time we were together, you didn't seem to mind being in my arms and staring dreamily into my eyes."

She scowled. "Because I realized the horrid mistake of allowing you such liberties last night."

Adrian cocked his head, studying her face. He must change her mind and make her realize the kiss they shared was not *horrid*, nor a *mistake*. "You cannot tell me you didn't enjoy what we shared in the pantry, because I know differently."

"That was last night, and I was… caught up in the moment. Today I realized I was wrong to let you do that to me. As I told you last night, I'm not that type of woman."

He loosened his hold and studied her pretty blue eyes that looked everywhere but at his face. "Tell me, my sweet Bridget, would you rather be with the Earl of Hanover right now, in his arms and kissing him the way you kissed me?"

A loud gasp sprang from her throat and her eyes widened. Before he knew what was happening, she slapped him across the face.

He released her and stepped back. Perhaps he'd deserved that. Although he had been wondering if she would rather be with his brother, he probably shouldn't have spoken his thoughts aloud. However, at least she was looking directly into his eyes, as he had wanted.

But what startled him more than the slap was seeing her injured expression. Anger was one of the emotions displayed, but her eyes watered as she blinked rapidly. Her lips trembled and her breathing quickened.

"How dare you say that?" she spat. She took a ragged breath.

"You told me last night that you respected me, and now you make me sound like I'm a… a…" Her voice broke.

Tears slid down her cheeks, tearing his heart to pieces. He groaned in silence. *I'm such a fool!*

Why had he been so mean? It wasn't his intention to hurt her. He actually hoped that she wanted to be with *him* and not his brother. But he couldn't stand seeing her so sad. The more tears that streamed down her cheeks, the guiltier he felt. A lump of emotion formed in his throat, making it difficult to swallow.

"Forgive me, my sweet Bridget." He took her back into his arms, but she slapped at his chest. He deserved it. However, he didn't know how else to let her feel his sorrow right now. "Please forgive me for saying that."

"Why… did you?" More tears filled her eyes.

He shook his head. "Jealousy. That's the only reason I spoke so rudely."

She blinked as surprise washed over her face. "You were *jealous*? Of whom?"

"My br… um, my cousin, the earl." Adrian couldn't believe he'd almost slipped up and given away his identity. He needed to stay in character a little better. Then again, lying to her was getting harder and harder.

"Why? Because he danced with me last night? Because he introduced me to your aunt and Lord Walden?"

"That, and because…" Adrian cleared his throat. "Because Lord Hanover was planning on coming to see you this morning. Collin mentioned he wanted to ask permission from your father to court you."

She gasped again, but now it was anger coating her expression. Usually when ladies found out a wealthy earl wanted to court them, they acted differently. Adrian wasn't prepared for her reaction, and he couldn't help feeling very confused.

Her face reddened and she scowled. "This was the reason you wanted to meet with me? To keep me away from the house so that Lord Hanover couldn't call on me?"

Feeling ashamed, he nodded.

She shoved her palms against his chest and squirmed out of his hold. "I can't believe…" She paced in front of him. "Of all the low-down tricks and deceitful games…" She growled, walking faster. "I blame myself. I knew men like you were scoundrels, yet I still allowed you to charm me."

Adrian scratched his head. Was she talking to him? She wasn't looking at him, but he was definitely the subject of her tirade.

"Um, Bridget? Why do you think I'm a scoundrel?" Her words didn't make any sense. They had only just met yesterday morning, yet she had *known* he was a scoundrel?

She stopped and faced him. Her glare shot right through him.

"Because you *are* a scoundrel, Lord William. I'm certain the things you have done to me since we first met were probably right out of the scoundrel's book of rules. In fact, you probably wrote the book."

Forcing a chuckle, he flipped his hand dismissively through the air. "I don't know where you are hearing such gossip, but I have never—and will never—become a scoundrel. True, I've done some inexcusable things in my life, but calling me a scoundrel is going too far."

She arched an eyebrow, folding her arms across her chest. "Did you even hear what I just said?"

"Of course I did, and I must disagree with you. Scoundrel is a harsh word, even for me."

Her breaths came fast as her nostrils flared. The quick tapping of her foot matched the rhythm of her finger tapping on her forearm. He couldn't possibly figure out why she acted this way.

His mind replayed what she had just said… and then came to a screeching halt. Had she called him *Lord William*? His heart dropped. Indeed, she had called him by his name, but all he heard was that he was a scoundrel.

He laughed uncomfortably. "Oh, I see. You believe me to be Lord William?" He shook his head. "Once again, you've been listening to too many rumors, my sweet Bridget."

"So, now you think I listen to rumors? Have you forgotten how I berated my sisters for gossiping yesterday morning while in your yard?"

"Well, no, I haven't forgotten, but—"

"Then it's obvious that you don't know me at all."

"But don't you see? I do want to know you better." He sighed and moved toward her, hoping to touch her hand, but the glare she gave him warned him to keep his distance.

"Well, Lord William, I'm not certain I want to know you now. I can see that *you* don't listen to rumors. After all, you and your brother moved into the estate hoping not to run across any social-climbing women, yet most of the unmarried women around here are not wealthy. You told me at the ball that you were trying to keep all of the farthing filchers away from the earl. But that's most of the women around this area. So, don't act surprised when I tell you I'm one of them."

He narrowed his gaze. She was still referring to him as William, so perhaps he should confess the truth. She must have overheard something during the evening to make her think he was Collin's brother. Either that, or innocent Aunt Beatrice could have said something.

He arched an eyebrow. "You are admitting that you are only after the earl because of his wealth?"

"As I just said, Lord William, don't pretend to be shocked. Lady Margaret was probably the only one at the party who doesn't need your family's money." Bridget shrugged and faced the pond, peering down at her reflection in the rippled water. "Anyone around here will tell you how desperate women are to find a man who can provide well for them and their family. Especially the Hartwell sisters."

He chuckled. "Desperate, you say? Oh, I beg to differ."

She turned away from him and walked slowly toward the clearing. "You can differ all you'd like. I have lived in this area a long time, Lord William, and so I know the women better than you do."

He hurried to her and grasped her elbow. "Please, Bridget. Stop calling me Lord William. I want you to call me Adrian."

"Is that your middle name?"

"Well, yes, but why—"

"But most people refer to you as William, do they not?"

He could keep the secret from her no longer. Nodding, he folded his arms. "I don't know who told you, but indeed, I am Lord William Worthington."

Scowling, she shook her head as her eyes glistened with unshed tears. "I cannot fathom why you would want to lie to me and everyone you have met in our small township, but I can assure you, the game you played with my heart will not be forgotten."

She moved toward her horse, and he followed.

"Forgive me, my sweet Bridget, if I offended you in any way. That was not my intent."

She threw a glare at him over her shoulder. "And what exactly was your intent? Why did you think it necessary to lie?"

Sighing heavily, he frowned. "I didn't want women to think I was in the marriage market."

"Truly, my lord, you went through a lot of deceiving to get that point across, when all you had to do was be honest when talking to women."

He took her arm, stopping her, but once again, she pulled away from him.

"I beg you, please forgive me." His chest clenched. He did not like the sadness buried deep in her expression.

"The way I feel now, I don't see that forgiveness forthcoming, but I shall promise to consider it."

"I'll cherish your promise. However, for now, I would beg you to keep my secret. I don't want people to know I live in the manor yet."

"I suppose, since it is not my secret to share." She lifted her chin stubbornly.

"Will you tell me how you know my identity?"

"I actually didn't know, but I suspected. There were small

hints along the way." She narrowed her gaze on him. "Were you aware that your aunt enjoys talking about her nephews who were at the ball? She is proud of them, more so even than her own son. Not once did she mention your name. Then, last night, when I asked her what the earl's brother looked like, she was more than willing to give me your description. Of course, it wasn't until today when my head finally cleared that I started putting together the pieces of your deceitful puzzle."

His mind went blank, and his heart hammered. No wonder she'd been so irritable. Yet she, too, had been keeping a secret from him, about her only wanting Collin because of his money. Part of him wanted to blame her for not being honest with him about her true purpose with landing a wealthy husband, yet… he was the one who had started the game of dishonesty. Perhaps he shouldn't be so hard on her.

"It would appear I am the bigger fool now," he said in a low voice.

"Indeed, you are."

She moved to her horse and prepared to mount, but he touched her arm, stopping her again. "Before you leave, will you promise me something else?"

"My lord, I would think one promise from the irate woman you lied to should be your limit."

"Just keep my secret for a few days longer. I assure you, it won't be long before the real Lord William returns to Hanover Hall."

Laughter bubbled up in her throat as she shook her head. Moving effortlessly, she quickly mounted and adjusted the reins in her hands. "I fear, my lord, that there would be no reason to tell anyone your secret. Everyone knows that I don't like to gossip. Remember?"

She kicked the horse and rode off before he could stop her again. Irritated, he fisted his hands by his sides. Not often did he meet a woman who could turn the tables on him, but it appeared that Miss Hartwell was playing him at his own game.

Well, he would have to ensure she didn't win.

Chapter Seven

ADRIAN HAD BEEN an utter nincompoop, and he didn't like feeling this irritated knowing he hadn't pleased a woman. Never in his life had he been rejected in such a way.

Usually, all he had to do was kiss the woman, and she melted into his arms. It had always been his habit to leave them after a few days or even weeks, and not think about them again. However, he didn't know how to take Miss Hartwell's blatant dismissal.

After he left her at the pond a week ago, he'd been determined to remove her from his mind. But many times, in the middle of the night, he would awaken after having a dream about her, and his chest would hurt with anguish. Men shouldn't have to suffer in such a way, and he was determined to forget about their time at the ball.

It wasn't as easy as he thought. Knowing the path where she and Collin traveled during the morning rides they'd been taking, Adrian had chosen that particular time to exercise his newest horse. He had tried to keep hidden so not to hear his brother's lectures later in the day about spying on them, but Adrian couldn't seem to stay away.

When he rode into town, he would always see Bridget or one of her sisters. How was he supposed to get the woman off his mind now? She was like a fungus that wouldn't go away. And those brief times he thought about moving out of the town entirely, a heaviness settled in his chest, and he knew he had to see her on a daily basis whether it frustrated him or not.

During the times he saw Bridget out in the open, she acted as though she didn't notice his presence, but he knew differently. Although their gazes hadn't met, her back stiffened and her expression tightened. He didn't need to be the most intelligent man in England to know she acted that way because of him.

Her attitude toward him should have kept him away. Indeed, her subtle refusal should have made him seek out other women to charm. Instead, it did the complete opposite.

Each morning, he waited for his brother to leave the house, and Adrian quickly saddled his horse and followed. As he waited in the thicket of trees near her home, he watched in anticipation, fidgeting in his saddle as though he stood on an anthill. It was as if he had some ailment or addiction. He couldn't wait to rest his eyes on the loveliest woman he had ever met.

In essence, he was a pathetic man, and he didn't know the cure. Yet waiting for the moment he would see her each morning came with moments of guilt. Although he tried pushing them aside, it had only made his mood worse.

Now, he sat atop his horse, watching through the trees as Collin, Bridget, and one of her sisters sat on a blanket in a meadow, having a picnic lunch. Adrian studied the oldest Hartwell sister, who still seemed to be stiff and proper. Of course, Collin had never tried to touch Bridget, except those times when he helped her up on her horse.

Something seemed off about the whole situation. Bridget was finally being courted by a wealthy man with an impressive title, yet her eyes didn't sparkle when she looked at Collin, not as Adrian recalled happening when he had held her in his arms. Her laugh seemed forced, as well. He received the impression that she wasn't enjoying herself, and since she and Collin had been together nearly every day this week, one would think the woman should act differently around the earl by now.

Adrian wanted to think that she still desired him and not his brother, but then he scolded himself for those improper ideas. These thoughts would only prolong his yearning for her, and he couldn't have that.

Sighing, he closed his eyes and rubbed his forehead. This insanity needed to stop. He should just give in and let his brother have her. Why would Adrian want a woman who didn't return his feelings? Then again, he didn't know why he felt this way. Indeed, he had gone mad.

Behind him, the leaves rustled and the ground crunched from the sound of a horse stepping into the alcove. Adrian sucked in a breath of panic and swung around on his saddle. The sun shone on the rider, momentarily blocking Adrian's view from the person interrupting his solitary afternoon.

The rider chuckled, and immediately, Adrian recognized the voice. He sighed heavily, letting his shoulders relax.

"Trey," Adrian groaned, "what in the blazes are you doing sneaking up on me like that?"

Trey rode out of the sunlight and stopped his horse beside Adrian's steed. The grin on his face was sickening, because Adrian knew that Trey had caught him spying on Bridget, which was quite embarrassing.

"I thought to pay you a visit, but your butler mentioned you had ridden this way." Trey shrugged. "I had nothing better to do than to find you, however..." He arched an eyebrow. "I'm dying to know why you are secretly watching your brother with Miss Hartwell."

"You know Miss Hartwell?"

"No, but at the ball, Judith noticed you chatting with the lovely miss, and my sweet wife decided to find more information about the maiden." Trey's lips twitched as though he struggled not to laugh. "I must say, I'm shocked that you are spying on the two. If you are that interested in the lady, then pay her a visit. Your brother hasn't asked for her hand in marriage yet."

"How do you know that?" Adrian tried to keep his mind

focused.

"Because I know your brother is also paying visits to two other women in the village." Trey shrugged. "Actually, my wife discovered that yesterday and told me about it."

Adrian shook his head and maneuvered his horse around to leave the thicket of trees. "You don't understand," he said over his shoulder as his cousin followed. "Miss Hartwell is not interested in me at all. She loathes my very presence, in fact."

"Impossible," Trey said with a bit of humor in his voice. "All women adore you."

Adrian rolled his eyes. "No, they don't."

He didn't want to sound arrogant and confess that most women *did* give him doe eyes whenever he was nearby. But he didn't care about those women. Only Bridget. He wished he knew *why* he only cared about her and not the others. The only explanation was that insanity had taken over his mind.

"So tell me, my good man," Adrian quickly added before his cousin could continue this awkward conversation. "What brings you to my manor?"

Trey rode side by side with Adrian. "I hope you have invested in some of Lord Hawthorne's speculations, because a few of them paid off. If you indeed invested, then you will be a wealthy man very soon."

Adrian should be overjoyed at the moment, and although he smiled at his cousin, it was difficult to feel the full effect of the wonderful news. "I was wise and invested. I'm happy to know your friend came through for me."

"Hawthorne came through for both of us." Trey grinned. "Being the youngest brother, I also need to rely on my friend for good advice."

"Then we shall drink a toast to our successful venture once we reach the manor and can pour glasses of port."

Trey laughed. "It's too early in the day to start drinking, my good man, and you had better not take up the habit. You'll never find a wife that way."

Adrian snorted. "I'm not looking for a wife."

"Indeed?" Trey motioned with his hand in the direction from which they'd come. "That is not what it looked like to me."

Adrian tightened his fingers around the reins and grumbled under his breath. Curse his cousin for pointing out the obvious, but a double curse on Bridget for making Adrian act this way.

"If you must know," he quickly tried to explain, "I act this way because I'm looking out for Collin. Miss Hartwell is not the right woman for him."

Another laugh burst from Trey, who exploded into fits as he tried to catch his breath. Adrian scowled. His cousin didn't need to have *that* kind of response, and the more Trey laughed, the angrier Adrian became.

"Oh, my good man." Trey shook his head. "You are being very humorous today."

"You think I'm lying?"

"On the contrary." Trey took a deep breath as his laughter subsided. "I think that *you* believe you're telling the truth." He shook his head. "My good man, have you forgotten how Judith and I fell in love? I too denied my feelings for the longest time."

If Adrian's anger grew any worse, he feared his head would explode. Not very often did he and this particular cousin disagree, and this was one of those times Adrian wanted to punch the man in the face. But he wouldn't. He would save that for his brother.

Exhaling slowly, Adrian tried to regain his control. "I fear, dear cousin, that your head is filled with foolish ideas. I'm sure that happens to every man who falls in love and marries, but I assure you, I do not have feelings for Miss Hartwell… unless, of course, they are feelings of guilt." He nodded once, coming to the realization. "Yes, that is what I'm feeling. Guilt."

Trey pulled his horse to a stop, which made Adrian do the same. Trey's eyes narrowed and a serious expression crossed his face.

"Guilt? Oh, Adrian. What have you done?"

Adrian wasn't certain he wanted to confess everything. "Let's just say that something happened at the ball last week that shouldn't have happened."

Trey's face tightened. "You didn't... take her virginity, did you?"

Adrian rolled his eyes. "Absolutely not. Give me some acclaim for having control over my desires."

His cousin's shoulders relaxed as a deep sigh escaped his mouth. "Well, thank goodness for that." He tilted his head. "Did you just steal a kiss?"

"Actually, I didn't *steal* anything. However, as I was trying to hide from Aunt Beatrice, I ran into Miss Hartwell. And, well... when she heard my aunt calling for Lord William, I knew I had to hide Miss Hartwell with me, so we hid in the pantry."

A loud gasp ripped from Trey's throat. "The two of you were in the pantry?"

Adrian nodded. "Nothing should have happened, but she wouldn't stop asking me questions, and the only way to silence her was..." He shrugged. "Needless to say, she was very cooperative while we were in the pantry."

Trey's humor returned, and he laughed loudly. "Forgive me, but I can't control myself."

"I wish you would stop laughing at my expense."

"But you look so... serious."

"I *am* serious!"

"But you have never felt guilty for kissing a maiden, yet now, you have guilt written all over your face." Trey laughed harder. "Oh, my good man. You are, indeed, smitten."

"Believe what you will, but I only want what is best for her and my brother." Adrian turned his horse toward the manor. "And I know Miss Hartwell well enough that I can say Collin is *not* the man who will make her happy."

"I'm quite certain you are correct."

As Adrian rode toward the manor, he didn't want to look at his cousin. That man had made him angry today, and he would rather not take out his frustrations on his favorite cousin.

Once they reached the estate, Trey made excuses why he couldn't stay and visit, which suited Adrian just fine. He wasn't in the mood for company anyway.

After changing his clothes, he went into his study and sat at his desk to read the letters he had received. Just as Trey had told him, there was a letter from Lord Hawthorne to tell him the good news. Still, it was difficult for Adrian to feel the excitement that he had made some money on his own. His father would be shocked, and Adrian couldn't wait to see the old man's expression when he told him the news. But even that didn't make him completely happy. A woman by the name of Bridget Hartwell had cursed him. Or bewitched him.

The latter was easier to believe.

Sighing, Adrian leaned his elbows on the desk and rested his forehead against his hands. The pounding in his head grew worse each day. Of course, if he didn't spy on his brother and Bridget, perhaps his headache would disappear. Yet seeing her every day made the heaviness in his chest a little lighter. As much as he tried to stay away, he couldn't. He was weak in the worst way, and he wished he knew how to stop it.

Seeing Collin's cheerful smile as he talked about his outings with Miss Hartwell didn't help Adrian's mood, either. He wondered if his brother did this because he knew how upset Adrian became. After all, the two brothers hadn't ever gotten along well.

But Adrian noticed that Collin *wasn't* doing it out of spite. The earl clearly enjoyed himself whenever he went to Bridget's house. There was a certain spark to his eyes that Adrian had never seen before. Now, whenever he saw that look on Collin's face, his chest tightened that much more. He feared that it would one day kill him. If that didn't end his life, seeing Collin and Bridget married would certainly do the trick.

The slamming of the front door brought Adrian out of his thoughts. From the corridor, the sound of grumbling grew louder. Curious, Adrian moved away from his desk and walked out of his study. Collin hobbled down the corridor, his clothes disheveled, his riding boots and knees coated in mud. Just above his right knee was a large rip in his breeches.

Limping and still grumbling, Collin made his way toward the stairs. Adrian hurried to assist his brother.

"What in the blazes happened to you?" he asked as he took his brother's arm, allowing Collin to lean on him.

"That, dear brother, is a most excellent question, one that I hope to find the answer to immediately." Collin shook his head. "I was returning home from my picnic with Miss Hartwell and her sister and felt the saddle shift beneath me. Before I knew what was happening, the saddle slipped off the horse, taking me down to the ground." He pushed his fingers through his hair. "I'm surprised I wasn't more gravely injured, since the horse came within inches of stepping on my leg."

Adrian stopped his brother on the stairs. "Did you feel the saddle slip during your ride to Miss Hartwell's house?"

"No, I don't believe so. I actually had other things on my mind, so if the saddle slipped, it wasn't enough for me to notice."

"I fear our stable hands have been lax in their duties."

"I agree, but it's more than that," Collin grumbled.

Adrian scowled. "What could be worse?"

"The saddle girth," Collin began softly as he glanced down and then up the stairs before looking back at Adrian, "was purposely cut."

Adrian hitched a breath. "Are you certain?"

Collin gave a sharp nod. "I've been around stables long enough to know what a worn saddle girth looks like compared to one that has been cut on purpose."

Adrian motioned toward the upper floor. "Come. Let's get you to your quarters. I'll send for a physician to look at your leg."

"I'll be fine. It's just a sprain."

Slowly, they moved up the stairs. Collin didn't speak, which gave Adrian time to think, and with this kind of information, thinking wasn't a good thing. If the saddle had been tampered with, did that mean someone on their estate was trying to harm the earl? Or what if it wasn't someone at the estate? What if someone from the neighboring land had snuck into their stables during the night and cut the saddle girth?

Or... what if it was someone that he or Collin had upset since they moved into the manor? Adrian couldn't think of anyone off the top of his head. The only people he had gotten to know since living here were a few servants and the stagecoach drivers from the handful of times he had gone to meet Trey and traveled to Manchester. But what of Collin? Had he angered anyone?

Adrian dismissed the thought. The only activities his brother had been doing of late were those that involved wooing a fair maiden—or two—and trying to decide which one he wanted for a wife.

He helped his brother to his bedchambers and directed the valet to take care of him. Adrian hurried back down the stairs, taking two steps at a time as he gripped the handrails. About four steps from the bottom, the handrail cracked. As he took the next step, the handrail broke apart.

Stumbling, Adrian managed to regain his footing and not topple down the remaining stairs. His gaze locked on the broken pieces of the handrail.

How very odd. The railing had not been wobbly yesterday that he could recall. He hoped there weren't more surprises from this old manor. Of course, it would explain why his father had paid such a low price for it. But the beauty of the place was enough reason to pay for its upkeep.

Carefully stepping to the bottom floor, Adrian kept his eyes on the railing. He studied not only the floor where the broken pieces had fallen, but also the steps where he had first felt the railing give away.

On the fifth step from the bottom, at the back of the crevice, was some sawdust. He frowned and peered back at the railing. It hadn't broken off until the fourth step.

His stomach rolled as realization hit him. This was *not* an accident. Whoever had tampered with the saddle had been inside the house, too. This wasn't a coincidence at all.

Chapter Eight

TEN DAYS HAD passed since the ball at Hanover Hall, and the earl had been to see Bridget almost every day. During his visits, they walked around her family's farm and the surrounding countryside. They discussed their likes and dislikes. She was grateful that one of her sisters—usually Priscilla—came with them, because Bridget feared they would run out of things to talk about. She also worried that the earl would bring up the subject of his wayward brother and see firsthand that Adrian was one of her major dislikes. Of course, then the earl would want to know why, and because she couldn't confess her sins, she would have to lie.

Pa would say she was going to hell. Thankfully, he didn't know, either.

Every day, Bridget waited for the earl to become bored with her or annoyed with her mischievous sisters, Felicia and Jannette, but he laughed at their antics and chatted with them as if they were longtime friends. If only Bridget could feel that way about the earl's brother, but it still upset her whenever she thought about it, which was more often than she wanted.

It was difficult, but she tried not to wonder why Adrian hadn't shown his face around the farm since their talk at the pond, and his absence gave her time to reflect on the anger still boiling inside. As the days passed, so had the irate emotion. Of course, she had been hesitant to forgive him for lying and treating her the way he had when they were at the pond, but at least now she didn't hate him or loathe his very presence. Perhaps that was because she hadn't seen him for a while.

Yet there were times in town, or while riding with the earl, when she *felt* as though Adrian was watching her. She tried to shrug it off, but the prickles of awareness still crawled over her body. If he hadn't been watching her from afar, why else would she feel that way?

By midafternoon, she was restless, and sewing on her sampler just could not keep her entertained. Lord Hanover usually came to visit around this time, anyway. It wasn't that she looked forward to his visits, but at least it was something to do. However, it was hard to laugh with him because when she looked into his eyes, they were the same hazel color as Adrian's, and they sparkled in the same way. How could she not think of Adrian when that happened? But she learned to look away whenever Lord Hanover laughed.

Bridget set her sampler down and picked up her mystery novel. But after reading two pages and not remembering one word, she gave up and placed the book on the side table. Deciding to prepare refreshments for Lord Hanover's visit, she walked into the kitchen to boil the water for their tea. Earlier today, Priscilla had made some crumpets in preparation for the earl's visit.

As Bridget moved back toward the parlor, Jannette and Felicia rushed into the house, laughing so hard their faces were red. Bridget studied their attire. Both girls had dirt smudged on their dresses, and their messy hair caused her to worry.

"What have you two been doing?" she asked in a high voice.

The girls exchanged glances and muffled their laughter behind their hands.

"Nothing," they chimed in together.

"I would hope," Bridget said quickly, "that you are not doing something Pa would get upset over."

"Not at all." Felicia shook her head. She nudged Jannette, and they darted up the stairs toward their room.

"Strange behavior," Bridget muttered as she walked into the parlor. But then, her sisters were only in their sixteenth and seventeenth years. Perhaps they were still too young to act with decorum. Bridget then realized their behavior was actually typical for such silly girls.

She stopped at the window and peered outside. Rain clouds were gathering in the east, and she prayed it wouldn't pour until after she and the earl returned from their walk. Being inside sipping tea and eating cakes was absolutely boring. It was as if nobody knew what to talk about.

Suddenly, the door slammed, and footsteps pounded on the floor. Bridget spun around just as Priscilla stomped into the room. Lines of irritation creased her sister's forehead and around her mouth. She appeared as disheveled as Felicia and Jannette had been, but thankfully, not as dirty.

"Where are they?" Priscilla's voice was louder than normal.

"I can only assume that you are referring to our *adorable* younger sisters."

Priscilla rolled her eyes as she marched toward Bridget. "Do you want to know what those two *adorable* girls did this time?" She held up a slingshot, and the long strings hung over her fingers and fell nearly to the floor.

Bridget held her breath, not really wanting to know what had happened. She knew her sisters well enough. They were always up to some kind of mischief.

"They dressed the Gosmans' sheep in Miss Tamara's corset!"

Closing her eyes, Bridget groaned. "Let me guess," she muttered, peeking at her sister. "Our sisters talked Miss Tamara into giving them her corset, again, so that they could dress the sheep in the latest fashion?"

Priscilla gave a sharp nod. "Oh, but it's worse than that."

Bridget nibbled on her bottom lip. Did she *want* to know what could be worse? "Does it have something to do with the slingshot?"

"Indeed." Huffing, Priscilla propped her hands on her hips. "After they dressed the poor sheep in the corset, they used the slingshot to shoot a rock into the bush where the sheep was grazing. It scared the poor animal so badly it began jumping all over the field. I made Felicia and Jannette help me catch it… and wouldn't you know, that was when Lord Hanover drove by in his carriage." She rubbed her forehead. "I know he saw us. It would be difficult not to see such a display. And I'm certain it absolutely appalled him. I mean, what titled lord would want to be married to a woman with sisters like *that*?"

Bridget rubbed the back of her neck, trying not to get too upset. She couldn't jump to conclusions. "Did you actually see Lord Hanover in the carriage?"

"Yes, and his attention was on me as I ran after the sheep. When Felicia and Jannette saw the coach, they darted in another direction and ran into the thicket of trees, laughing loudly."

"Oh dear." Bridget moved to the cushioned chair and sat. Pa was not going to like this one bit.

"Do you know what this means?" Priscilla's voice lifted higher.

"I can only imagine," Bridget muttered, and closed her eyes again.

"Thanks to our wayward sisters, the earl will have nothing to do with us. He will be too embarrassed to come around. In fact, I wouldn't doubt he is considering how to tell Pa that he has decided that the two of you don't suit."

"Yes, I know." Sighing, Bridget looked at her sister, waiting for sadness to come over her from the knowledge that she had lost another beau. Yet the feeling hadn't come yet.

Priscilla set the slingshot on the side table. "Just when you get your chance at being courted by a titled, wealthy man, our sisters have to ruin it." Her voice cracked.

Bridget scowled. "Prissy, do you honestly believe I care that he's titled *or* wealthy?"

A blush covered Priscilla's face. "Um, no, but…"

"Because I'm not. The amount of money in the man's bank account has nothing to do with how I feel about him."

Priscilla took cautious steps closer and sat on the edge of the empty chair. "Bridget," she said in softer tones, "exactly how do you feel about Lord Hanover?"

"Well, I…" Bridget prepared her thoughts, and was surprised when nothing was there. She really didn't know her feelings. She liked him well enough, and she was happy when he visited, but it was only because it kept her from becoming bored. If the man wasn't in her life, she would have found something else to do to entertain herself during the slow part of the day.

"I suppose I… um…" Bridget began again, still grasping for words, but then she heard her father clear his voice loudly. She snapped her attention toward the door to the parlor, and her heart sank. Standing beside her father were none other than the earl… and Adrian.

She sucked in a quick breath. *What is Adrian doing here?*

Both Bridget and Priscilla jumped to their feet at the same time, but it was Priscilla who smoothed out her dress and patted her messy hair.

"Forgive us for not seeing you." Bridget curtsied, and her sister copied the action.

Her father motioned for the other two men to enter. When they reached Bridget and her sister, the men bowed.

"It is good to see you again," the earl said. He pointed to Adrian. "I would like to introduce you to my brother, Lord William. He has finished his business, and he is permanently residing at Hanover Hall." He looked at Adrian. "And this is Miss Bridget Hartwell, and her younger sister, Miss Priscilla."

Priscilla gasped and quickly covered her mouth with her hand. Her eyes were wide as she stared at Adrian.

The earl chuckled. "I'm assuming by your reaction that you realize my brother was at the ball we had not too long ago."

"Yes, my lord. If I'm not mistaken, he chatted with Bridget a few times."

"Forgive me," Adrian said. "It was my request to remain unnamed while at the welcoming party. I hope you will understand."

"Um… of course, my lord." Priscilla's hand trembled as she ran her palm over her dress again, smoothing out the wrinkles that would remain there until the garment was ironed.

Adrian kept his gaze on Bridget, and for the oddest reason, her heartbeat quickened with a strange fluttering. Quickly, before her mind changed toward the rodent masquerading as a man, she squashed the disturbing feelings.

"Miss Hartwell, it's a pleasure to see you again," Adrian said.

Bridget kept her shoulders straight. "And you, as well. I'm happy to know you have decided to let everyone know your real identity." She tried to keep her voice from shaking.

"Indeed." Adrian grinned. "I thought it was about time now that my business has been settled out of town."

"Would you like some tea?" Priscilla asked. "And I made some fresh crumpets this morning."

"That would be wonderful." Adrian nodded.

"Please, why don't you sit with us?" Bridget motioned with her hand toward the two chairs. The men sat as she and Priscilla poured tea in the cups and served them the cakes. Pa sat next to the two lords, his attention focused on the men.

"I'm very happy that I wasn't at the church preparing the sermon today when you came by," Pa said. "My daughters tell me you have come to visit them every day since the ball."

Collin nodded, smiling brightly. "Yes. I find your daughters delightful company. They make me laugh more than my dreary brother does."

As the others chuckled, Bridget held back from snorting. The earl found her *delightful*? Why would he think their boring conversations were delightful? Unless it was her other sisters he actually came to see, because Bridget was not *delightful* company at all.

After a few seconds passed with nobody talking, Bridget had to break the silence. "Lord William," she began after sipping her tea. "You mentioned having business out of town. May I be so bold to ask what type of business you are in?"

The smile stayed on his face as he set his teacup on the coffee table in front of them. "I have invested stocks in steam and coal. And just the other day, I was in Manchester with a good friend of mine setting up a warehouse to make cotton."

"How incredible." Pa's eyes were wide as Adrian had his full attention. "If you are looking for workers, there are some men in my congregation who are not employed. They would be very dependable, I assure you."

Adrian smiled at her father. "I would very much like to meet these men. I'm always looking for dependable people."

Pa puffed out his chest. "I shall let them know."

Bridget was surprised that Adrian actually did something with his life—besides seducing innocent women and creating deceitful games to toy with their hearts, of course.

"I agree with my father," she said. "I'm impressed with your investments as well."

Collin turned to his brother. "I've been thinking lately about investing in the cotton business along with you. Perhaps you could introduce me to your friend."

"Of course. It's cousin Trey's brother-in-law, Lord Hawthorne." Adrian lifted his teacup from the coffee table and sipped.

Collin lifted his eyebrows. "Indeed? I know Hawthorne quite well."

"I believe I know this man." Pa tapped his finger on his chin. "Does he live in North Devon?"

"Indeed, he does, but he also has an estate in Manchester," Adrian replied.

"Yes, I do know him." Pa grinned. "What a humorous man, I might say."

Adrian chuckled. "That is a good way to describe Hawthorne. Half the time I never know if he is serious or playing the fool."

Bridget arched an eyebrow. She'd known that feeling well since meeting Adrian.

"Miss Hartwell, Miss Priscilla," Collin said, "would you ladies enjoy going horseback riding with my brother and me? We brought some fine mares from our stables that I think you two would love to ride."

Priscilla's face reddened. "Oh, I don't know." She stroked a hand down her messy hair. "I'm really not presentable."

"Nonsense." Collin smiled. "You look lovely. Doesn't she, Lord William?"

"Of course you do." Adrian nodded. "There's nothing to feel embarrassed about. After all, by the time we all return from our ride, I'm sure we'll all have scuffed up boots and windblown hair, since the wind has picked up a notch. In fact, I'm willing to bet you'll be just as pretty when we return."

Priscilla laughed lightly and shyly looked at her hands on her lap. Bridget narrowed her gaze on Adrian. Was he purposely trying to charm her sister? Apparently, since he couldn't charm the eldest Hartwell sister, he might as well try the next one in line. Well, Bridget would *not* allow it. She didn't need all of the sisters ruined by one man.

"Shall we be off, then?" Collin stood.

Bridget and Priscilla rose to their feet at the same time. Adrian turned to place his teacup on the side table, but it bumped against Bridget's mystery novel, knocking it to the floor. She hitched a breath and bent to retrieve it, but Adrian beat her to it and lifted it from the floor. As he handed her the book, his hazel eyes twinkled.

"Miss Hartwell, is this your book?" he asked as a corner of his mouth twitched.

"It is." Bridget took the book and held it protectively against her bosom.

"I'm happy to see you're a fan of mystery novels."

"Indeed, I am."

"Are there other books you enjoy reading as well?"

She really didn't approve of the way he looked at her as if they shared a secret. And she absolutely didn't like the way she became captured by his intense stare every single time. It must be his remarkable eyes. What other reason could there be?

"I like reading many books, my lord." She nodded.

Priscilla moved closer to Bridget. "Oh, but mystery books fascinate her, which is why you'll see her reading them often."

Adrian arched an eyebrow as he stared at Bridget. "What do you find so fascinating?"

"I suppose it's trying to figure out the mystery as I'm reading. I enjoy being surprised at the end when I don't suspect the ending."

"Are you any good at solving the mysteries?"

She nodded. "I think I'm very good at it, actually. Not many books keep me wondering until the end."

Adrian grinned wider. "You know, that doesn't surprise me at all. From the little we talked at the ball, I felt that you were that type of woman, Miss Hartwell."

With an uncomfortable laugh, Bridget placed the book back on the side table. "Yes, well… shall we go riding now?"

"I'll fetch our shawls." Priscilla hurried into the corridor near the front door.

"Pa?" Bridget asked. "Will you be joining us?"

"Not this time, my dear." Her father stepped to her and kissed her cheek lightly. "You and Priscilla enjoy yourselves with these two honorable men."

Honorable? Bridget nearly choked from the thought. Collin was honorable, but certainly not his brother.

Priscilla returned with the shawls, handing one to Bridget. It surprised her when Adrian assisted her sister with the shawl. Irritation boiled inside Bridget, and she gritted her teeth. If he were trying to make her jealous… well, he was wasting his efforts. She would just show him that it didn't bother her in the least that he was paying attention to Priscilla—as long as that was all he did with her sister.

Holding her head high, Bridget hooked her hand around Collin's arm as he led the four of them out of the house. Determined not to let Adrian's actions affect her, she decided to dote on Collin's every word and every breath.

Two could play at the jealousy game.

Chapter Nine

"WHAT EXACTLY GOES into running a farm?" Adrian asked, riding his horse closer to Priscilla's.

Bridget kept her attention on her giggling sister as the woman's cheeks reddened. Her younger sister was playing right into Adrian's hands. Bridget tightened her fingers around the reins. She was sure that that particular Worthington brother enjoyed making innocent women blush. He certainly lived up to his title of *scoundrel*, even though he had tried to argue with her about being called that.

"Oh, Lord William." Priscilla shook her head. "I'm sure you don't want to know everything that my sisters and I do."

"Yes, of course I do. Please, enlighten me."

Adrian gave Priscilla a smile, the same smile that always made Bridget weak in the knees. She would have to ask her sister later if her heart ever fluttered whenever Adrian was around, because Bridget wished hers would stop reacting to the man in such a way. If only those feelings of anger and resentment hadn't stayed with her. Perhaps the absence of not seeing him made her think differently. No, that couldn't be it.

As Priscilla began explaining what the sisters did on the farm, Adrian kept his gaze intently on her. Bridget was relieved that he at least appeared to be interested in farm life, although she knew he was good at pretending.

The earl rode up next to Bridget and grinned. He nodded toward the other two.

"It appears," he said in a low voice, "that my brother has finally become interested in someone besides himself."

Bridget couldn't hold back the laugh that sprang from her throat. She quickly covered her mouth with her hand. Adrian glanced at her briefly before returning his attention to Priscilla.

"Forgive me, my lord," Bridget said to the earl, "but that was very amusing."

Collin's smile widened. "But it's the truth."

"I can't help but wonder," she continued in soft tones, hoping Adrian couldn't hear, "if your brother is really that way or if it is an act to ward off upstart women."

He chuckled. "I can tell you know my brother well in just the little time you conversed with him at the ball."

Panic filled her, and she nodded. "Yes. I believed him when he spoke to me that evening as he pretended to be your penniless cousin."

"Then can you honestly tell me that you didn't think he was arrogant and cocksure of himself during your conversation?"

She tried not to laugh this time, though it was a struggle. "I must confess, when I first met him, it was several hours before the ball had started. My two younger sisters were trespassing on your land, and he presented himself as your cousin at that time. I found him very arrogant, but at the ball…" She shrugged. "He seemed to change, but only slightly."

Collin's eyebrow arched. "Change? How so?"

"He was sweeter and didn't seem so self-absorbed." Bridget wasn't about to tell him that Adrian had only acted *sweet* while they were hiding in the kitchen's pantry. However, it was his charm that had trapped her.

Collin released a heavy sigh. "My brother has been judgmental when it comes to social classes. He had his heart injured by a woman who only wanted him because of the Worthington family's money, and since then, Adrian has hardened his heart. I hope he wasn't too rude to you."

"No, he wasn't too rude. Nothing I couldn't handle."

As she studied Adrian still pretending to be intently listening to Priscilla, Bridget's heart started to soften. Had he truly allowed a woman into his heart—enough to hurt him? For some reason, that seemed impossible. But if that was what really happened, then it was no wonder he had lied about his identity when they first met.

Blowing out a pent-up breath, she realized she couldn't allow this to alter her decision about him. He was still a scoundrel.

The crunching of wheels behind them drew Bridget's attention to the buggy slowly coming their way. Collin stopped his horse, and she pulled the reins to stop her animal, too.

"Good afternoon." Aunt Beatrice was driving the one-horse buggy toward them, waving. "I hope you don't mind if I join you, Lord Hanover. When your valet told me that you and Lord William had gone to take the Hartwell sisters riding, I knew I had to come along."

Collin nodded. "Of course, Aunt Beatrice. We would love your company."

He glanced at Bridget as if waiting for her approval, so she quickly smiled at the older woman. "Of course. It'll be nice to chat with you once again."

Suddenly, a blast like a pistol firing ripped through the air. Before Bridget knew what was happening, Collin clutched his shoulder and fell from his mount. Bridget's horse reared up. She grasped the reins firmly, trying to calm the animal and bring it under control, but the mare continued to dance around. Seconds later, her mare bolted away from the others.

Bridget cried out and clung to the reins, trying to tighten her leg around the horn of the sidesaddle. She leaned closer to the horse's neck as fear rushed through her. *Oh, Lord. Please help me!*

EVERYTHING HAPPENED ALL at once, and Adrian didn't know who to help first. His brother was holding his shoulder, but since he could see there wasn't a lot of blood, he knew Collin would be fine.

Priscilla screamed her sister's name.

Without another thought, Adrian dug his heels into the flanks of his horse and urged the animal into a gallop, racing after the runaway mare. His heart pounded with the same rhythm as the horses' hooves as they galloped toward Bridget. Pain gripped his chest, and he prayed that she wouldn't be thrown to the ground.

"Come on… go faster," he snapped at his horse.

The gap between him and Bridget was closing, but not quickly enough, in his opinion. Finally, when he was at last able to maneuver his horse beside hers, he reached out to her. "Take my hand."

Wide, frightened eyes looked at him. Her face had lost color, and her lips were tightly pressed together. She shook her head.

He guided his horse a little closer. "Bridget, take my hand. I won't let you fall."

Tears filled her eyes as she shifted her attention between his hand and her horse.

A thicket of trees loomed ahead. If they rode in there, he wouldn't be able to make this move. It had to happen now.

"Trust me, Bridget." He leaned forward, stretching his arm toward her once more.

She met his gaze, and for a moment, there was a look of confidence on her expression. She released the reins and reached for him. Leaning closer, he wrapped an arm around her waist and yanked her off the saddle. Her arms flew around his shoulders as she hung on to him.

He quickly reined in his horse as he pulled Bridget in front of him. She linked her arms around his neck and buried her face against his chest. The moment his horse stopped, he circled his arms around her, pulling her tighter in his embrace.

Her whole body trembled, and it nearly killed him to know

she could have been seriously injured. Breathing deeply, he tried to quell the panic that had risen inside him as he rested his face in the crook of her neck.

"Oh, Adrian." Her voice shook. "I thought… I thought…"

"Shush, my sweet. I wouldn't have let anything happen to you." He brushed his lips over her neck. "You are safe with me."

She stayed against him as he stroked his hands over her back, trying to calm her the best way he knew how. Slowly, the trembling in her body subsided and she sighed heavily.

"What happened back there?" she asked, lifting her head to look into his eyes. Her arms dropped from around his neck.

"I wish I knew." He caressed her cheek, wiping away a few tears. "But I thank the good Lord that you are safe now."

"What…" She looked over his shoulder in the direction where they had been. "What happened to your brother?"

"I believe he was shot."

She sucked in a quick breath and met his gaze again. "*Shot?*"

"Yes, but I think he is all right. He was knocked off his horse, but I didn't see very much blood before I took off after you."

"Oh, Adrian." She relaxed, laying her head on his chest again. "I've never been so frightened."

"Neither have I." He kissed her forehead, keeping her in his arms, relishing the warmth their bodies shared at this moment.

Several minutes of silence passed between them. Closing his eyes, he inhaled her intoxicating flowery fragrance. Suddenly, the memory of them in the kitchen's pantry filled his thoughts. He would never forget her unique scent.

"Adrian? I think we should return to the others." She pulled away and looked into his eyes. "I'm certain they will want to know about my welfare."

Indeed, they should return, but he didn't want to let her go. He didn't want to stop staring into her lovely blue eyes, either. "Yes, we should get back."

A shaky smile came across her face. "Th-thank you, Adrian. You… risked your life to save mine."

He cupped the side of her face. "I would do it again if it meant seeing your heart-melting smile once more."

Her face went red, and she dropped her gaze to his chest. "I... thank you, my lord. I don't know how to repay you."

"Please, call me Adrian," he whispered. "Hearing my name from your angelic lips is the only thanks I require."

She lifted her gaze again, and her smile grew a little wider. His heartbeat hammered so fast that he was certain she could feel it too. Dare he hope he was finally softening her heart toward him? Would she finally forgive him for lying?

She twisted on his lap and faced forward, which was her silent request to return to the others. Without another word, he guided the horse back around and headed toward where they had left Collin, Priscilla, and Aunt Beatrice. Adrian purposely rode his horse slower just to spend more time with Bridget.

Even though he couldn't see her face, at least he could smell her enchanting scent. His arm stayed around her waist, holding her against him.

For now, this would do. But soon, he would want more. So much more.

Chapter Ten

BRIDGET PACED THE floor in the sitting room, wringing her hands against her middle. She should be worried about Collin and check on him to see if his injury was healing from where the bullet grazed his shoulder yesterday. Yet the earl was not on her mind. Instead, her thoughts were kept busy replaying every minute… every earth-shattering second that she had been with Adrian once he rescued her.

She had been so afraid, but the look of determination in Adrian's eyes when he reached for her gave her comfort. She had hesitated to trust him, but when she took the chance, he came through for her. The realization rattled her, and she hadn't known how to act.

Perhaps she shouldn't have clung to him the way she did, or let him hold her so tightly or kiss her forehead, because the feelings she had wanted to squash, from when they were in the pantry the night of the ball, had returned in full force. While he comforted her on his horse, her body came alive with memories, reminding her how much she had enjoyed the way his hands stroked her back, and the way his muscular chest felt against her palms. She recalled his manly scent of leather and spice, and his soft expression as he caressed her cheek. When he brushed his lips across her forehead, she longed for that moment with him in the pantry, kissing him so passionately.

But it had been so very wrong then, and it was certainly wrong now—especially since his older brother was practically courting her, although he had yet to speak with her father and make it official. Part of her hoped it didn't happen, but the other part of her knew she needed to marry a wealthy man.

The scent of biscuits wafted through the air, and her mind became alert. Gasping, she rushed into the kitchen, scolding herself for not remembering she was making biscuits. Priscilla stood by the stove, taking out the long pan of freshly baked treats. Bridget sighed, grateful that her sister's thoughts were not preoccupied.

"Did you get the basket ready?" Priscilla asked sweetly.

Inwardly, Bridget groaned. Apparently, her mind was all over the place today. "I forgot, but I shall get to it now."

She moved to their small pantry and took down a basket from the shelf. Immediately, her thoughts moved back in time, putting in her in another pantry and in a very handsome and charming man's arms…

Stop it! She wished these memories would fade, because they disrupted her life too much.

Bridget wiped out the basket and placed inside a newly embroidered cloth that Priscilla had been working on yesterday when the girls planned to take biscuits to the earl. The shooting incident had shaken everyone. The earl had tried to pass it off as if someone was pheasant hunting and a stray bullet had grazed his arm, but Bridget thought differently. She had been with her father and some of the men from church when they had gone hunting, and she knew what a close-range pistol blast sounded like. Whoever pulled the trigger hadn't been too far away.

She glanced outside the window and watched the drizzling rain. Perhaps they should postpone their call on the Worthington brothers today because of the weather. Then again, she had been hesitant to go to Hanover Hall anyway. Just thinking about seeing Adrian again made the nerves in her stomach flutter.

"Do you think we should wait for tomorrow to take the

basket of biscuits?" she asked her sister.

Priscilla's expression fell in disappointment. "Why would we wait?"

Bridget motioned with her head toward the window. "Because of the rain."

Prissy moved her attention to the window before returning it to Bridget. "It's not raining that much. We shall be fine."

Although Bridget wanted to feel upset because they were still going, excitement raced through her, making her heartbeat quicken. She really needed to figure out how to stop this feeling. There was no use acting this way when nothing good could come out of it. It didn't matter that Adrian had been sweet yesterday when he rescued her—he was still a scoundrel of the worst kind.

Or was he?

Bridget shook her head. No man could change that drastically.

Felicia walked into the kitchen and straight to the biscuits that Priscilla had carefully arranged in the basket. The younger sister reached for a biscuit, but Priscilla slapped Felicia's hand and glared.

"These are not for you."

Felicia arched an eyebrow. "There is no need to become so mean. I only want one. I don't think your precious earl will miss one biscuit."

"If you must know," Priscilla snapped, "our *precious earl* and his brother are very kind neighbors, and it would be foolish to not appreciate the attention they have been giving to our family."

Felicia held up her hands in surrender. "Forgive me for being hungry." Her gaze moved to Bridget. "Do you feel the same way about our neighbors?"

Bridget hesitated, only because she struggled with answering honestly. "They have had plenty of opportunities to reject our friendship—no thanks to you and Jannette—but the Worthington brothers continue to show their kindness."

There. That wasn't a lie.

Felicia laughed heartily and shook her head. "You two women are doe-eyed, and it's most humorous to see you both tripping over yourselves to please the earl and his brother."

Bridget wanted to tell her sister how wrong she was, but she held her tongue as the younger sibling walked out of the kitchen.

Priscilla finished with the basket and placed the remaining cloth over the top of the biscuits. She looked at Bridget with a skeptical expression.

"Do you think Felicia is correct?"

"About what?"

"About us being doe-eyed for the lords?"

Bridget chuckled and hoped her cheeks didn't grow too hot—enough to notice, anyway. "Absolutely not. Our sister forgets that this has never happened to us before, and, well… it is rather nice to have the attention from the Worthington brothers, even if I don't believe it will last long."

"You don't?" Priscilla stepped closer. "Why not?"

"Neither of us has a dowry, so I don't see the lords offering marriage."

Priscilla released an audible sigh and frowned. "I thought of that as well, but then I wondered why the Lord Hanover keeps coming to see us if he isn't interested, and why did he introduce us to his brother?"

Bridget shrugged. "I wish I knew." She motioned with her hands toward the door. "Are you ready to leave?"

"Yes, after I fetch my cloak."

It didn't take long before Bridget and her sister were in the family's chaise. Priscilla held the basket as Bridget took the reins and guided the horse toward Hanover Hall. Thankfully, it wasn't raining hard, but the weather had turned chilly. She still wondered if staying home would have been the best decision to make today, but Priscilla was anxious to get the freshly baked biscuits to the Worthington brothers.

Bridget's stomach twisted. She feared her sister had feelings for Adrian. Of course, the man had shown what a charming gentleman he made, even if she thought he wasn't being truthful. She would have to be ready to console Priscilla when the scoundrel showed his true colors and broke her heart. Bridget prayed that he didn't try to steal kisses from her sister as he had done with her. If that happened, she wouldn't hesitate in blackening his eye with her fist.

A small voice in her head tried to tell her she wasn't being reasonable. *To err is human, to forgive divine.* How many times had her father repeated this phrase? Even in his sermons, he talked about forgiving those who had trespassed against them.

Would she finally be able to get Adrian from her thoughts if she forgave him? There was only one way to find out... If only she could bring herself to forgive.

"You are quiet this morning," Priscilla said.

Bridget shifted in her seat. "I'm sorry. I don't mean to be."

"Is there something on your mind that you wish to share?"

Bridget nearly laughed loudly. If Priscilla only knew. "Nothing at all."

Priscilla touched Bridget's arm. "You have been quiet since the ball at Hanover Hall, and I'm worried about you."

Holding her breath, Bridget scrambled to find things to say. She didn't want to lie, but neither did she want her sister to know what had really happened at the ball.

"I'm sorry you are worried," Bridget said. "But you shouldn't be."

"Are you hoping the earl makes an offer of marriage?"

Bridget swallowed hard. Once again, she didn't know how to answer. She really should confess her feelings. She had always shared her secrets and dreams with her sister, and it truly wasn't like Bridget to keep this bottled inside.

"Well, to be perfectly honest—"

Suddenly, the carriage tilted as the wheel hit something hard. Pricilla cried out, bracing one arm against the wall while her other arm held tightly to the basket. Bridget stiffened and tightened her grip on the reins. When the vehicle leveled, it wobbled terribly. She pulled the reins, stopping the horses.

"What just happened?" Priscilla asked.

"I'm not certain, but something is wrong with one of the wheels."

"Do you think we ran over something?"

"I do, but what could possibly make the wheel so rickety afterward?"

Priscilla shrugged. The poor woman's eyes were wide with fright and her face was pale.

Bridget scooted forward on the seat, preparing to get out, but her sister grasped her arm, stopping her.

"Where are you going?" Priscilla shrieked.

"To see what is wrong with the wheel. There is no way I dare drive the rest of the way to the manor if the wheel is damaged." She released her sister's hold and patted her hand. "Don't fret. I shall be fine."

She opened the door to the carriage and carefully stepped down. The muddy road would probably ruin her boots and the hem of her day dress, but sitting inside the conveyance wouldn't accomplish anything.

The clouds hid the sun, and the trees created shadows across the carriage, but one thing was certain—one of the large wheels in the rear had been broken. She was correct in assuming that traveling to the manor would have only made it worse, and the vehicle might overturn. It was better that they stop now.

"What do you see?"

Priscilla's worried voice came from the carriage, and Bridget looked toward her sister peeking out through the open door.

"The wheel is broken."

"Oh dear." Priscilla placed a hand to her bosom. "What should we do?"

"We need to walk."

"*Walk?* In this weather?"

"What other choice do we have?" Bridget pointed up the road. "We are closer to Hanover Hall, so we should walk there and beg the earl to allow one of his servants to fix the wheel."

"Oh, I don't know." More color left Priscilla's face. "Would the earl think we are being too forward by asking for help?"

"Prissy, I think the earl would think us foolish if we didn't ask for help." She reached out her hand. "Give me the basket and I'll help you down."

The look on Priscilla's face let Bridget know her sister was not happy about their outcome. She realized that if only she had followed her instincts to not come today to check on the earl, they wouldn't be in this predicament. Then again, her father would have been driving the carriage otherwise, so perhaps it was better that they were this close to someone who had the means of giving assistance so that their father didn't have to worry about it.

Once Priscilla stood beside her, they linked arms and made their way toward the manor. Bridget absolutely abhorred walking with her feet so muddy, but it must be done. Perhaps this would be the turning point with Adrian—or the earl. As soon as they notice how filthy the two sisters were, the lords would probably turn up their noses and not want to see them again.

Good riddance, Bridget thought. Then again, what if the lords' reactions were just opposite?

No, she couldn't think of that.

The closer they came to the manor, the faster they walked. Bridget didn't know who had picked up the pace first, but her wet feet made her colder. When they finally reached the manor's front door, her teeth were chattering. She knocked hard, wishing she could stop trembling.

Thankfully, the butler answered the door moments later, and as he scanned both Bridget and Priscilla, a look of disgust crossed his features. Bridget fisted her hands. Couldn't the imbecile see that they were in dire straits? After all, what respectable woman would visit a lord looking like a drowned rat?

"We beg the intrusion, but our buggy broke a wheel," she told the servant. "Can we speak with the earl or his brother?"

The older man arched an eyebrow and opened the door

wider, motioning with his hand for them to enter. Keeping hold of her sister's arm, Bridget made certain they didn't walk too far into the hall with their mud-coated boots.

He closed the door and haughtily lifted his chin. "If you'll wait right here, I will fetch one of them."

"Yes, of course," she muttered, trying not to say anything rude, especially since visitors were supposed to be shown into the parlor to wait. But in this case, staying by the door was best.

"Oh dear," Priscilla whispered. "We have upset the butler. That cannot be good."

"Even if the servant doesn't understand, I'm certain the earl or his brother will."

Priscilla blinked with wide eyes. "I pray you're correct."

Bridget shrugged. "If I'm not, then we'll discover today how snobbish the Worthington men really are."

In a way, she hoped Adrian would show his true colors. Then again, she wasn't sure what his true colors were. Was he indeed the scoundrel she thought of him as, or the kind man who'd rescued her from the runaway horse?

She rubbed her hands together, trying to warm them up. Even wearing her riding gloves, they were still cold. But the heat coming from the fireplace in the nearby room helped warm her, even if it was just slightly. At least her teeth weren't chattering any longer.

Fast footsteps were heard coming down one of the corridors, and immediately, Bridget straightened her shoulders. She may appear like a waif, but she refused to act like one. Yet when she spotted Adrian hurrying toward them, the beating of her heart took on a different rhythm.

As he neared and his gaze moved over both Bridget and her sister, his expression was the opposite of that of his servant. Worry was the look on Adrian's face, and she sighed with relief.

"What has happened?" he asked, stopping in front of them, reaching out to take Bridget's cold and wet hands.

"Lord William," she said as she started to curtsy, but Adrian held her up, not allowing her to do the proper show of respect. "Please forgive our appearance. On the way to bring you a basket of freshly baked biscuits, our buggy wheel broke and we had to walk."

"The wheel broke?"

For some reason, Adrian acted surprised that it was only the wheel. What else was he expecting? Then again, after what happened yesterday with his brother, he probably suspected more.

Bridget nodded. "Just the wheel, my lord." She licked her suddenly dry lips. "I'm hoping we can beg you for the use of one of your servants to help fix it. I know it's a lot to ask, but—"

"Absolutely." He looked over his shoulder. "Gilbert? Please come here."

The butler walked briskly toward them. "Yes, my lord."

"Please have one of the men in the stables fetch the Hartwell sisters' buggy and bring it to the manor, then instruct them to fix the wheel."

"As you wish, my lord." The butler nodded before hurrying toward one of the side halls.

Adrian expelled a breath and looked back at Bridget. "Now that we have taken care of one problem, let me see about fixing the second one."

She arched an eyebrow. "Second problem?"

"Yes. Your attire. You need to get out those wet clothes before you catch your death."

Priscilla chuckled. "As much as we appreciate your kindness, my lord, I don't believe you will have any clothing fit for a lady in your manor, since it is only you and your brother who reside here."

He smiled, meeting Priscilla's gaze. "You are correct. However, we have women as servants. As long as you don't mind wearing their uniforms, we can get your gowns cleaned up quickly."

"Lord William," Bridget said, gaining his attention once

again. "You don't need to put your servants through that extra work. After all, it was my fault that we came during a rainy day."

"We were only coming to drop off these biscuits"—Priscilla held up the basket—"and to see how your brother is faring after he was shot yesterday."

Adrian gave Priscilla a sweet smile and took the basket. "You are both so thoughtful to think of my brother and make him biscuits."

"Well," Priscilla said as her cheeks reddened, "you can have some biscuits as well."

Adrian laughed. "And I cannot wait to take my first bite. However, let's get you two taken care of first. I'll be back momentarily. I need to find our housekeeper, Mrs. Wendel. She'll get you two cleaned up and in some warm clothes."

After Adrian disappeared down one of the corridors, Bridget sighed heavily. Had she misjudged him before? Or was she just seeing him in another light?

"I must say," Priscilla whispered, "that I'm vastly relieved he didn't throw us out. But then, I knew he wasn't that mean." She narrowed her gaze on Bridget. "Which makes me wonder why you seem to think differently."

Bridget shrugged. "I suppose he has changed from when I first met him."

"Or maybe you are the one who has changed." Priscilla grinned. "After all, women in love act differently."

Bridget nearly choked on her gasp. "*In love?* Why would you think I'm in love? That's just utterly ridiculous."

Priscilla gave her a skeptical stare. "You aren't in love with the earl?"

Inwardly, Bridget groaned. Her sister was talking about Collin and not his brother. Goodness, Bridget really needed to follow the conversation more closely. Either that, or she needed to stop thinking about Adrian so much. But she had been trying, and look how far that got her.

Chapter Eleven

ADRIAN COULD TELL the sisters were uncomfortable sitting in the parlor, talking with him and the earl, wearing maid uniforms, but it was better than the alternative. Although he wouldn't mind seeing Bridget wearing nothing but a bedsheet, he doubted she would think the same. And even though he couldn't stop the images of what she would look like from popping in his head—with her hair hanging around her shoulders and down her back, making her appear so much more alluring—he certainly wouldn't want to see her sister in that manner.

Thankfully, Collin tried to make the situation better by chatting with them as if nothing had changed. Adrian was also very grateful that his aunt and idiotic cousin were kept in their chambers. Apparently, his aunt still suffered from the vapors after yesterday's upset with someone shooting at Collin.

Adrian instructed the housekeeper that neither she nor any of the maids were allowed to inform his aunt about their visitors. He feared that his controlling aunt might think it wasn't proper to have the Hartwell sisters here, wearing maid's dresses, while sitting with two lords near the hearth. In his opinion, the afternoon passed by smoothly, and he hadn't been so relaxed in quite some time. The only thing that could make this better would be if Collin and Priscilla weren't here.

Upon Bridget's request, Collin told stories about his and

Adrian's childhood. Adrian was relieved that the earl chose to make light of how two brothers grew up not getting along, which made the stories humorous. Adrian enjoyed watching Bridget laugh and the way her face lit up. He especially enjoyed the twinkling in her pretty eyes during this time. Perhaps that was why he felt so relaxed.

But another thing he liked about this afternoon was seeing the way Bridget looked at him. There was no anger in her expression, and no malice in her voice when she spoke to him. He could only hope that she didn't hate him any longer. Then again, he wondered if she did it for show. After all, his brother was courting her, and she needed to make a good impression.

Yet she had gotten so upset when discovering he'd lied to her. Would she do the same to his brother?

"Lord Hanover," Mrs. Wendel said from the doorway. "Could I have a word?"

Collin nodded toward the housekeeper before looking back at Bridget and Priscilla. "If you'll excuse me. I shan't be long."

"Of course," both sisters said together.

Collin stood and moved across the room toward the door. Bridget's gaze shifted to Adrian again. It had been doing that so much this afternoon. He didn't mind it at all.

"Do you think our clothes are dry?" she asked him.

He shrugged. "Perhaps that is what the housekeeper is talking to my brother about."

"No," Priscilla said, nudging her elbow against Bridget's. "It takes much longer for clothes to dry, even in front of a hot fire."

"You're not anxious to return home, are you?" He tilted his head, keeping his gaze on the lovely woman. "I was actually enjoying myself visiting with the two of you."

Bridget arched an eyebrow, and her expression told Adrian she didn't believe him. He wished he could make her trust him. If only he hadn't lied to her when they first met.

"We are enjoying our visit, too." Priscilla looked at her sister. "Aren't we?"

"Yes, of course. It's been a pleasant afternoon." Bridget smiled, still keeping her attention on Adrian.

Collin returned to his chair and sat. "Mrs. Wendel wondered if you two would be staying for the evening meal. I told her you would." He paused. "I hope that meets with your plans."

"Well, my lord," Bridget said, sitting on the edge of her chair as if she wanted to bolt, "we don't want to burden you any more than we already have. So, if our buggy is ready—"

"Of course it's not ready," Adrian quickly interjected, even though he didn't know for certain. "It's only been a few hours. Repairing a wheel takes much longer."

"It does?" Collin asked.

Adrian realized Bridget was looking skeptical again. He didn't want to lie to her any longer, which meant that he had to tell the truth, even if they left within the next hour.

"If you would like," Adrian said calmly, "I will check on the vehicle for you."

"Yes, please." Bridget nodded.

"Then, if it isn't ready," he continued, "will you stay and take the meal with us?"

Bridget glanced into her sister's pleading face, sighed, and looked back at Adrian.

"Yes, we will stay."

He smiled and stood. "Then I'll have Gilbert check with the stable hands to inquire about the progress of the wheel."

Although he tried not to rush out of the room, he didn't want to be away from Bridget any longer than necessary. Thankfully, Gilbert was in the kitchen, chatting with the cook. When the butler noticed Adrian, he quickly approached him.

"Gilbert, would you check on the Hartwells' buggy?"

"Yes, my lord."

"Thank you." He turned to leave and spotted one of the kitchen maids. "And will you check with Mrs. Wendel to see if the Hartwell sisters' clothes are dry?"

"Of course, my lord." She curtsied.

Adrian took fast steps until he neared the parlor before slowing his pace. He didn't want to look as anxious as he felt.

As he walked into the room, the first person to look his way was Bridget. His heart skipped a beat, and he grinned. Keeping his gaze on her, he moved to his chair and sat.

"I'm having our servants check on the wheel as well as your clothes." He winked. "But I must express my hope that they are not ready, only because I'm not willing to say goodbye."

"I must concur with my brother." Collin nodded. "Which, I might add, rarely happens."

They all chuckled, even Adrian. His brother couldn't be more correct.

"Well, you both have been very hospitable." Bridget smiled. "I've never met kinder men in my life."

Adrian held his breath. Did she really mean that?

"It's only because we enjoy the company of such lovely ladies," Collin said. "And we hate to see you go."

"Pardon me, my lords." Mrs. Wendel stepped just inside the parlor, gaining everyone's attention. "The ladies' clothes are dry, but their buggy is not yet ready."

Slowly, Adrian released a sigh of relief, hoping it wasn't noticeable. Bridget wouldn't be leaving yet.

"So, what do you say?" Collin asked her. "Will you and your sister stay for the meal?"

She nodded. "We will be happy to."

"Miss Hartwell, Miss Priscilla, if you would follow me," the housekeeper said, "I'll take you to change back into your clothes."

As the women stood, Adrian and Collin jumped to their feet until after the pair left the room. Collin walked to the decanter of port on the side bar and poured himself a glass.

"Do you want a drink?"

Adrian shook his head. He didn't need spirits tonight. Having Bridget here, looking at him with sparkles in his eyes, was enough to have him floating around the room. "No. I'm fine, thank you."

"I must say"—Collin took a sip of his port—"that you are

different."

"Different? What do you mean?"

"Whenever I've seen you with women, you are charming, but self-centered. Never have you volunteered to do something nice for them. Yet, in the past two days, I've witnessed you going out of your way to do things you don't normally do. Yesterday, you rode after Miss Hartwell when her horse was out of control. If you had seen that happen a month ago, I doubt you would have been so bold. You would have given the reason of not rescuing the maiden because it would have gotten dirt on your new clothes. And today, you took in two women who were muddy and wet, and instructed the stable master to repair the wheel on their vehicle. The old Adrian would have had one of the servants take the women home without offering any assistance."

Adrian rolled his eyes. "You have a very low opinion of me, and you always have. Just because I have done some selfish things in my life doesn't mean I'm always selfish. And because we have never gotten along and stay away from each other as much as we can, I assure you, the man you describe is nothing like the man I was." He didn't want to admit that his brother was close, though.

"Then forgive me. However, that doesn't change the fact that you have changed since we moved here. Perhaps the country life agrees with you after all."

"Perhaps." Adrian walked to the door and peeked into the hall. Of course, the women wouldn't be changed yet. But chatting with his brother wasn't as enjoyable.

"In fact," Collin continued, "I think I know what brought on this change."

Shaking his head, Adrian faced his brother. "And what, pray tell, would that be?"

"I think you are falling in love."

Adrian snorted a loud laugh. "In love? Are you addled? Why would I fall in love with a penniless country woman?" After he said it, he glanced behind him, hoping Bridget wasn't nearby and overheard. Thankfully, as he suspected, they were not dressed yet.

"I believe one of Hartwell sisters has captured your interest. I think it doesn't matter if they are poor farm girls—you like them anyway."

Sighing heavily, Adrian crossed his arms and walked toward the window. This topic was ridiculous, and he wished they would change the subject quickly. "Not to worry, brother dear. I'm not in love."

Collin chuckled. "That's not what our cousin Trey thinks."

Adrian spun around. The feeling of betrayal came over him. How dare his favorite—his *ex*-favorite—cousin say that about him? "Trey is up in the night. His love-struck wife is too nosey for her own good. But Trey is wrong, and so are you."

Collin poured himself another drink. "Then tell me why you haven't excused yourself by now and left? You have had all the time to leave the room, yet you stay and continue to share stories with the Hartwell sisters. Why is that, I wonder?"

Adrian rolled his eyes again, tired of his brother's overactive imagination. "Because I'm bored. I have nothing else to do but visit. I cannot go riding because of the rain, and playing cards with you isn't something I like doing."

Collin snickered. "If you say so, brother."

"Of course I say so. You heard the words come from my mouth, so why wouldn't they be true?"

Collin tilted back his head and laughed boisterously. "Trey was right. You are in complete denial."

Grumbling, Adrian marched toward the door. "I'm going to check on the meal."

Both his cousin and brother were wrong. Terribly wrong. He was *not* in love with Bridget. Of course, Collin never did name the Hartwell sister he believed Adrian was supposed to be in love with, but it didn't matter. He was enamored with Bridget, but he wasn't in love. Eventually, another woman would catch his eye, but until that happened, he was satisfied in Bridget. After all, he still wanted to kiss her again, and while that thought was foremost in his mind, how could he think of charming another woman?

BRIDGET STARED AT herself in the mirror as one of Adrian's maids styled her hair. She wasn't certain she liked someone else touching her hair and helping her dress. But, if by some odd chance, she became Lord Hanover's wife, she would be expected to have many servants waiting on her constantly. How did titled women keep from getting bored? Already, just watching the maid in the mirror was quite tedious.

Priscilla had been taken to the next room to change. Bridget couldn't understand why they wouldn't allow the two sisters to be together. At least she would have someone to talk with, but she didn't know the servant well enough to converse. Then again, she hated sitting doing nothing but watching.

"I hope you don't mind my asking," Bridget began, getting the maid's attention in the mirror, "but what is your name?" The servant didn't appear to be that old. Perhaps in her early twenties.

Her eyes widened, clearly surprised at Bridget's question. "Emily Fransen."

"What a lovely name." Bridget smiled. "Emily? How long have you worked for the earl and his brother?"

"I started working for their father three years ago. When the brothers moved into Hanover Hall, I was assigned here."

"Do you know Lord Hanover and Lord William well, then?"

"I suppose I know them well enough." Emily giggled. "At least, I know their bad habits."

Bridget chuckled. "Yes, I'm sure being a servant and cleaning up after them would let you hear juicy details about their lives."

Emily shrugged and continued arranging Bridget's hair. "Actually, I learn things from the valets and footmen. They hear so much and are willing to share with the rest of us. However, everyone at Hanover Hall is devoted to the Worthington brothers."

"Is there something about the brothers you would like to share with me?" Bridget really shouldn't encourage the maid to gossip, especially since she was against it. However, if they were talking, Bridget wouldn't become bored and fall asleep in the chair.

The maid blushed a brilliant red.

"Oh, Miss Hartwell. I couldn't possibly. I hear talk, and both Lord Hanover and Lord William are taken with you."

Bridget groaned silently. *Both?* "You and I both know that a titled man is not going to marry a country woman with no dowry. I don't know why Lord Hanover is still courting me, but I can assure you that he will not ask for my hand in marriage."

Emily sighed and frowned. "You are correct, of course. I haven't known any titled lord who married a woman without a dowry."

Bridget couldn't understand why her chest was tightening. Yet she hadn't gotten her hopes up… or had she? Why would she do something silly like that?

"There you go," Bridget said. "I'm just being used for entertainment until Lord Hanover can find a titled woman."

"Or perhaps"—Emily paused, staring at the wall—"maybe he finds you so very different from the women who come from titled families, and he likes you for your sweet personality." Her gaze met with Bridget's in the reflection. "After all, you are nothing like some of the women I have met in London."

"I thank you for your flattery, but I assure you, once he is bored with me, he will move on." Although they were speaking about Lord Hanover, she pictured Adrian. Indeed, that man would become bored soon and move to the next unsuspecting woman. He might be charming now, but if she let her heart get involved, he would surely break it.

"That is certainly the habit of Lord William. It doesn't take him long to move to the next conquests. However, Lord

Hanover is more selective. Rarely does he only court one woman."

Bridget nodded. If that were the case, Adrian would soon give up on her. She didn't know whether to be elated or saddened by the news.

Emily stepped back to look at her creation. Bridget took this moment to glance out the window. The rain had stopped. It was time to return home, whether they had a vehicle to take them or not. She didn't enjoy lying to people, but in this case, she needed to feign a headache in order to return home. Her heart was in jeopardy, and she couldn't afford having it broken.

"I thank you for helping me change and style my hair." Bridget tried to smile at the servant. "By chance, do you know if my sister is ready?"

"I shall check, Miss Hartwell."

As the maid hurried out of the room, Bridget found her clean boots and put them on. She had promised both Lord Hanover and Adrian that she and her sister would stay, and she prayed they wouldn't judge her too harshly when she begged them to release her from that promise.

Bridget moved to the door, but before she could leave the lovely room decorated with mauve and gray, and the most expensive furniture she had ever seen, Priscilla bustled in and grabbed her shoulders. The wide smile on her sister's face and the gleam in her eyes let Bridget know that convincing her to leave would be impossible.

"Oh, I cannot believe any of this," Priscilla whispered. "Is this not the most amazing room you have ever seen?"

Expelling a breath, Bridget nodded. "Yes, this manor is very lovely. We are very fortunate to have this opportunity to view the inside. But, my dear sister, you must pull yourself out of the clouds." She stepped away from Priscilla, and when her hands dropped, Bridget grasped them. "We are but mere country girls. We do not have any chance of becoming Lady Hanover or Lady Worthington."

The excitement in Priscilla's eyes vanished as her smile sank. "I know, but it was nice to dream."

"Indeed, it's nice, but we should not expect much else. Soon, this dream will end, and we cannot fall in love with the Worthington brothers. Our hearts cannot take it."

"You are correct, again." Priscilla inhaled deeply, squaring her shoulders. "I know you don't want to stay, but can we at least live the dream during the meal? I'm starved."

It was as if Bridget's stomach had a mind of its own, because it growled. She groaned. Apparently, her hunger made the decision for her. "Fine, we'll stay. But after this, we need to return to our normal lives."

Priscilla nodded. "All right, we will."

As Bridget walked down the stairs with her sister, she wondered how she could bring Pa's mind out of the clouds. He still expected her to marry a wealthy man and save their farm. Things like that didn't happen in the real world.

Chapter Twelve

ADRIAN DRUMMED HIS fingers on the desk, not even paying attention to the ledgers in front of him. Today, he was not in the mood to conduct business of any sort. All he could think about was what had transpired this week with Bridget.

As if saving her from the out-of-control horse hadn't created fear inside him, his heart had melted from their visit after she and her sister's buggy broke down and they showed up in mud-soaked clothes looking like drenched waifs. He had tried to convince himself not to think about Bridget, to give her sister more attention, yet it hadn't worked out that way.

It had been a delight to have their company during the meal. However, Bridget acted differently than she had earlier that day. At first, he wondered if she was anxious to return home, but then he wondered if she had overheard his conversation with Collin, although Adrian didn't think it was possible. Yet Bridget was more reserved, and she didn't meet his gaze very much.

As they readied themselves to leave once the buggy wheel was repaired, Adrian was ready to offer his assistance to follow them home, but his insipid brother volunteered first, and the ladies accepted.

For fear of following in his brother's footsteps, Adrian waited only seconds after they all left before he had his horse saddled and rode behind at a distance so they couldn't see him. Once they reached the Hartwell farm, Collin had dismounted and walked the ladies to their front door. What irritated Adrian was when his brother kissed Bridget's knuckles as he told her goodbye. He had showered the other sister with the same gesture, but it still bothered Adrian that his brother had done that… when it should have been *him* kissing the back of Bridget's hand and gently stroking her fingers for the brief moments he held them.

Now, all he could do was think of her parting words to him before leaving the manor. The look in her eyes haunted him. He'd received the distinct impression that she was telling him goodbye forever. But that was ridiculous, since they both lived in the same town.

However, now he felt differently. For the past three days, Collin had tried to visit Bridget at her home, only to be told that she was under the weather. At first Adrian wondered if she had caught a chill from having to walk in the rain the other day, so he had ridden to their farm to spy on her, but when he noticed her through the window moving around and doing chores, looking very healthy, he knew she wasn't ill.

Grumbling, he pushed away from the desk and walked to the window. The sun was high in the cloudless sky, and this would be a beautiful day for riding—if he was in the mood. But being disheartened about Bridget's attitude had doused his excitement about being outdoors.

He must talk to her again, if only for his own state of mind. Yet would she accept him as a visitor at her home when she had been turning away his brother for three days? As he tried to decide what to do as the clocked ticked by the minutes, the yearning to see her again grew inside his chest, making it more difficult to breathe. He wanted to hear her laugh because it melted his heart. Instead of dreaming of her sparkling eyes, he wanted to watch them when she looked at him as if she had never seen anything so perfect—as she had done when he rescued her from the runaway horse. And God help him, he wanted to privately hold her in his arms and kiss her passionately. Of course, he needed to figure out a way to make that last part happen, since she was always with his brother or her sisters.

Then a thought struck him. The Worthington brothers could have a dinner social and only invite a few neighboring families. The evening would certainly be more relaxed than when they had the ball earlier in the month.

Before he changed his mind, he rushed out of the study and into the hall. He wasn't certain where his brother would be in this large manor, but for certain, Aunt Beatrice would know. Thankfully, her high-pitched voice was easier to hear than Collin's monotone.

Adrian followed the sound until he found his aunt in the music room, instructing Walden on the importance of learning how to play the pianoforte. The poor, mentally challenged cousin sat at the musical instrument with a blank look on his face. Walden had always been a mousy-looking man, and at the age of thirty, the pathetic bachelor's brown hair was thinning, and his cheeks appeared almost sunken. If Adrian didn't know any better, he would think his cousin was sickly, but Aunt Beatrice denied there was anything wrong with the man.

The woman paused in her lecture, but before Adrian could speak, Walden started playing a song. Adrian cringed. It sounded terrible. He hoped the man either found a different talent or only played for those people who couldn't hear well.

"No, no, no," Aunt Beatrice said loudly, causing Walden to stop. "You are not doing it correctly."

Walden released a frustrated breath as his shoulders sagged. Adrian felt the man's irritation, but he didn't have time to wait for the old biddy to continue with her lessons.

He quickly stepped forward and cleared his throat loudly, gaining the attention of the other occupants of the room. Walden appeared relieved for the interruption.

Aunt Beatrice smiled wide and came toward Adrian. "What a pleasure it is to see you this morning." She stopped in front of him and clasped their hands together.

"Forgive me for stalling my cousin's music lessons, but I have something to discuss with you."

"What is it?"

"I would like you to help me plan a dinner social with our neighbors. I only want a few families invited."

She gasped and linked her fingers together, bringing them up to her bosom, looking surprised. "You wish for *my* help?"

Adrian chuckled. "Well, since you have done this kind of thing before and I have not, you are the only one who can help."

"Oh, Lord William, I couldn't be more thrilled." Tears glistened in her eyes. "I shall have a wonderful meal prepared that will impress your country neighbors. You and your brother's social will be the talk of the town for weeks on end."

When she finally stopped talking, her mouth pursed, and her expression let Adrian know she was in serious thought. He didn't dare interrupt her, but neither did he want to wait for her to continue her plans. Now that he had given her permission to plan the evening, he wanted to leave and let her begin.

"I shall get you the guest list today," Adrian said.

She snapped to awareness and met his stare. "Splendid. I shall get started on it immediately."

"Ma?" Walden asked in a whiny voice. "Does this mean my lesson is over for today?"

"But of course," she snapped. "I have more important things to do now."

Adrian left the room, feeling almost sorry that his cousin had such henwit for a mother. But at least his own plans were in motion for when he would see Bridget next. She would not turn down the invitation, only because the whole family would be invited—even her boisterous sisters. Hopefully, between Mr. Hartwell and the eldest two daughters, they would be able to control the other two.

He went back into his study to work on the business ledgers, but as the day passed, Aunt Beatrice's shrieking voice jerked him from his thoughts more often than not. He was sure his servants would be relieved when the old woman and her son finally left Hanover Hall. Her absence would certainly remove strain from his life.

His grumbling stomach reminded him he hadn't eaten lunch, and if he wanted a clear mind to finish the ledgers, a full belly was required. He stretched his arms and yawned before pushing away from his desk and standing. The day was passing too slowly, especially when he anticipated the upcoming dinner social.

Earlier, when he put together the guest list for Aunt Beatrice, he'd made certain to invite families with eligible women, mainly to keep Collin's focus off Bridget so that Adrian could win her favor instead. He hoped to reignite the yearning way she had looked at him when he rescued her from the runaway horse. He anxiously waited to share a passionate kiss with her as they had done in the kitchen pantry.

It was also his hope that his talkative aunt would distract Bridget's father and sisters so that he could sneak Bridget away without anyone noticing. He hoped he could convince her that he wasn't the scoundrel she had labeled him, but instead a man who desired her more than any other woman. Although he'd done his share of breaking women's hearts in the last several years, he wanted to prove to Bridget that he had changed. Good grief, if his own brother noticed a difference in Adrian, surely he wasn't the same man as before.

He left the study, searching for his aunt to see how things were going with the party's plans. The woman's loud voice led him to the kitchen. She stood amongst some servants, issuing orders. Since her arrival, she had behaved as though she was the mistress of Hanover Hall, and it was her duty to keep the manor running smoothly. She had acted like their mother for as long as Adrian could remember, and although he'd repeatedly told her that he was a grown man and didn't need mothering, she continued to give it.

He rolled his eyes. Perhaps he shouldn't scold her yet. After all, if Adrian had his way, Aunt Beatrice would be instrumental in helping Collin find a wife—and it wouldn't be Bridget.

When the old woman saw him, her eyes widened, and a smile stretched across her face. "William, dear."

She bustled toward him. Her gray hair bounced on her head, and he feared it would soon come out of the coil she kept it in.

"William, I have everything under control." She tapped his forearm. "You need not worry. In two nights hence, the dinner social will go off as planned. In fact, the invitations have already been sent."

"I thank you, dear aunt. I knew it was wise to ask for your help."

Her cheeks bloomed with color. "But of course. Who else would be so knowledgeable in planning parties, especially at Hanover Hall?" She puffed her chest out like a proud peacock. "Now aren't you glad I haven't left yet?"

He dared not reply for fear she wouldn't approve of his answer. But for certain, after the party, he would inform her that she and her son had overstayed their welcome. With any luck, Collin would agree with Adrian, even though it didn't happen very often.

"You are certainly a godsend today." He grinned. "And I know this party will be a success."

She lifted a finger and pointed it at him. "Don't ever take dinner socials lightly. One never knows what budding romance might come from it."

He laughed. Leave it to his aunt to play matchmaker. She was determined to get *both* of her nephews married. He wished she would focus more on her own son instead of her nephews. Walden was an odd sort of man who, Adrian was certain, would never marry. What he could tell from watching his cousin during parties was that he repelled most women. In fact, many men couldn't even stand to play cards with Walden. Adrian suspected the poor man had been dropped on his head one too many times as a baby.

"Oh, Auntie, you are being very humorous," Adrian said

sweetly. "The only person residing in this estate who will marry is my brother, and I assure you, he already has a budding romance started. Two of them, in fact. But with your assistance bringing a few more women into his life, perhaps he will make up his mind and find the one who will be his wife."

Aunt Beatrice's mouth hung open as her jewel-decorated fingers flew up to her throat. "Lord Hanover is courting *two* women, you say?"

"Yes. He's been seeing Miss Hartwell, as well as Lady Margaret."

"Lady Margaret?" The older woman's forehead wrinkled more, if that were even possible. "But Lady Margaret is practically a *spinster*. And Miss Hartwell... Well, although she is a fine woman, she lives on a farm. She probably doesn't even have a dowry." She nearly spat the word, as if it didn't belong in her vocabulary.

Adrian shrugged. "Actually, out of the two, Lady Margaret is best suited, since her family has money. She is younger than Collin by a year. I assure you, the woman is marriage material. However, because of his reluctance to ask for the lady's hand, I fear that he has lost interest, which is why I am inviting other available women to the party for him to become acquainted with. But I need your help to convince him."

"Oh, pish." Aunt Beatrice flapped her hand in the air. "I'll make Collin see how foolish it is to court a spinster, and he'll find another woman to get to know." She tapped her finger on her chin. "But that doesn't explain why you have invited the Hartwell family."

He quickly thought up an excuse. "Because we don't want Collin to suspect our motives. You know how hardheaded he is."

"Indeed. I believe he gets that trait from me."

Adrian bit the inside of his cheek. He wasn't going to tell his aunt that neither he nor his brother had inherited anything from her. Collin had been making his own decisions since he was twelve. But as long as Aunt Beatrice was concentrating her efforts on Collin and not on Adrian, perhaps the dinner social would go off splendidly.

However, that just meant Adrian needed to hint to his brother to give the women his undivided attention, as long as it wasn't Bridget. He would convince his brother how rude it would be to single out one woman at the party. Maybe then Bridget would turn her focus to Adrian, and only him. He grinned. Now *that* would make a very pleasant evening.

Aunt Beatrice moved back toward the kitchen staff and continued explaining their duties for the dinner social. Adrian left the room to see if the servants had set out the meal yet, since he figured he wasn't the only hungry person at the manor right now.

As he turned the corner, he detected a woman's strong perfume. He stopped, inhaling the scent in the air. He frowned. That was a smell he did not know, especially as there were only a few women at the manor.

He listened for a woman's voice, wondering who could possibly have dropped by to visit without informing him, but he didn't hear anything. He moved to the nearby rooms—the parlor and the sitting room—but they were empty.

Shrugging, he decided he must be smelling things. After all, Bridget had been filling his mind of late, and he absolutely loved her fragrance. Perhaps that was why he detected a woman's scent. He would recognize her smell anywhere. *Lilacs*. He loved how her gentle fragrance had always put his mind on a dreamy cloud of bliss.

He continued down the corridor, and an eerie feeling washed over him. The hairs on the back of his neck stood. He stopped and scanned the spacious hall in front of the winding stairs. A noise from the second-floor landing caught his attention, and he jerked his gaze upward. Suddenly, a potted plant came flying over the railing, heading straight for him.

Cussing, he jumped out of its way just before it crashed to the floor. A mixture of dirt and plant scattered across the tile in a complete mess.

Blowing out an exasperated breath, he ran his fingers through his hair. *What is going on around here?* One thing was certain—this was not an accident. Another certainty was that Collin was not the only person being targeted, especially given his brother was nowhere in sight.

After being shot at the other day, Collin had contacted the constable. Both Adrian and his brother told him of the strange things that had been happening around the house. The constable acted as if the brothers were making up stories just to get attention. It had irritated Adrian that the so-called lawman hadn't taken them seriously.

Hopefully, now the man would. Everything that was going on was planned to hurt the Worthington brothers, and Adrian would not tolerate this any longer.

A clamor of footsteps shook the floor as servants and Aunt Beatrice ran toward him. When she reached him, she grasped his arm. Her gaze jumped between him and the broken potted plant.

"What in heaven's name…" Her wide eyes met his gaze.

"It fell," he said, not realizing his voice was shaky. "From up there." He pointed toward the stairs.

She glared at the nearest servant. "Go upstairs to see who did this. Make haste before they get away." She returned her gaze to Adrian. "I pray we won't have to postpone the dinner social." She shook her head. "Things are happening around here that are unexplainable, and I won't have rumors being spread through town."

Postponed? Although he understood his aunt's distress, the only thing that would calm Adrian's nerves now would be to see and talk to Bridget. Her sweet smile would help him in so many ways. Of course, her passionate kiss would be nice to have as well.

"No," he snapped. "The event will still take place. I won't hear of it being postponed." He glanced at the servants. "And *my* word is final."

They nodded, and most of them turned to go back to the

kitchen. Two servants brought brooms and dustpans to clean up the broken pot and plant.

"Adrian, my dear," Aunt Beatrice said, shaking her head, "I pray you are right. I don't know how well your guests will handle having something terrible happen during the party."

"Not to worry. I know what I'm doing." Of course, the first line of business would be to question all the servants, especially the ones on the second level. Someone must have witnessed something. He wouldn't believe otherwise.

Whoever was behind these incidents was in for a big surprise. The Worthington brothers wouldn't admit defeat. They would continue with their daily lives and pray that the person responsible was caught and punished soon. Of course, Adrian's reasoning for the haste was that having visitors at their estate would be dangerous until the culprit was apprehended. He didn't want to imagine Bridget's being injured because of something he or Collin had done.

Chapter Thirteen

BRIDGET WAS RELUCTANT to go to the party tonight, but her father was very insistent. It didn't help that Pa had pulled her aside yesterday to question her about how things were progressing with the earl. It hurt to do so, but she confessed her feelings—that titled men wouldn't marry a woman without a dowry.

Pa's anger had surprised her, but then she realized he was acting out because he knew she was right but wouldn't admit it. She waited patiently for his tirade to end, and when it did, he told her that the family would be going to tonight's dinner social, and that she would wear her nicest gown. Once more, he warned her what would happen to their family if she failed to get a wedding proposal.

Since then, she had been fighting tears. More than anything, she hated disappointing her father, but she feared this time couldn't be helped. Lord Hanover wouldn't offer marriage to her, and even if by some odd chance he did, she doubted she could honestly accept. She wanted love to be part of the deal, and for certain, she didn't have those feelings for Collin Worthington and never would. In fact, sometimes she wondered if Priscilla liked the earl more than her.

She did as her father requested and wore her best gown and had Priscilla style her hair. Her sister knew Bridget didn't want to go tonight, but thankfully didn't ask about it. During the carriage ride to the manor, she grew impatient for the night to be over with. Her sisters were anxious, just as they had been before the Worthington brothers' ball.

The vehicle stopped, and her father opened the door to help his daughters out, but he pulled Bridget aside before they walked up to the porch.

"I want you to know I'm proud of you and I love you." His throat jumped in what was probably a hard swallow. "And whatever happens tonight will be because it was meant to be."

She nodded. "Yes, Pa."

"But please promise me that you won't turn away the earl's attention."

"Pa, I haven't done so yet, and I don't plan on doing it. But as you said, whatever happens tonight is for a reason."

She hooked her arm around her father's elbow and walked beside him up the steps to the door. Immediately, it was opened by the butler. He nodded a polite greeting to her, and she gave him a smile.

The family was shown into the large sitting room. Already, some of their neighbors had arrived and looked their best. Of course, when invited to events such as this, it was expected to appear even better dressed than one would going to a wedding.

It didn't take long before the earl and Adrian came over to greet them. It seemed Adrian tried to beat his brother to her side, and although she wanted to laugh, she refrained.

"I'm pleased you could come," Lord Hanover said to her pa, "and that you brought your daughters." He turned to Bridget and took her hand before kissing her knuckles. "Miss Hartwell, I pray you are feeling better?"

"Yes, my lord. My health has improved." She pulled her hand away, but within seconds, Adrian was taking it and lifting it to his mouth. His lips felt more tender as they brushed her knuckles, and she felt the subtle stroke of his finger against her palm.

Tingles erupted inside her belly, creating warmth to spread through her. She hadn't felt this way when the earl kissed her.

The older brother had never been able to create such havoc inside her like his younger brother. If only she could marry a man who made her feel so special, and so desired. If only the man who could make her feel like a woman and asked for her hand in marriage would be wealthy enough to save her family's farm, perhaps she wouldn't disappoint her father.

It seemed as though time stood still while Adrian's lips touched her hand, and as he slowly straightened, his intoxicating hazel gaze locked on to her face. All sounds around her disappeared as she watched him carefully, hoping he wouldn't do or say anything to let everyone around them know of their secret.

The beating of her heart increased as the strength disappeared from her legs. It was all she could do to hold herself up and not embarrass herself in front of everyone. Adrian always had a way of charming her.

"Miss Hartwell, I'm so glad you came." He winked.

"Lord William," she said in a raspy voice, then quickly cleared her throat. "I thank you for inviting us."

"I wouldn't have it any other way."

Her heart skipped a beat. Was this dinner social his idea? Of course it was. He had always been the bigger flirt out of him and his brother. Leave it to Adrian to find ways for them to be together. The cad!

Although she suspected his intentions, it felt good to know that he hadn't lost interest in her yet. The maid had mentioned that Lord William quickly moved from one conquest to the next. Bridget found it refreshing that she had captured his interest for so long.

Her father's voice broke the spell as he asked Adrian a question. Being polite, Adrian moved his attention to her father as they conversed. Although she couldn't wrap her mind around the conversation, she did notice when Adrian glanced at her several times.

Inhaling deeply, she convinced herself that she would remain strong. His charm, good looks, and sweetness were *not* going to make her swoon, no matter how hard he tried.

As the evening progressed, she realized there was something different about Adrian. He seemed more relaxed and self-assured. There was more confidence in his manner and the way he spoke with the guests at the party. Whether it had something to do with his being Lord William now, as opposed to the country-bumpkin cousin she had first met, she wasn't certain. But she liked how kind he was to everyone. That was so different from the night at the ball.

Finally, the guests were invited to follow the brothers into the huge dining room for supper. Just as she found a card with her name on it, Adrian was by her side, pulling the chair out for her. She smiled and allowed him to help her sit, even though he *accidentally* swept his fingertips across her shoulder, making her shiver with delight from his touch.

He moved to pull out the chairs for her sisters, but Bridget noticed he didn't touch any of them. It was difficult not to watch him as he then pulled out chairs for the other ladies in attendance before moving to his seat and sitting. She wasn't surprised that his position at the table was directly across from her.

She really didn't want to look at him as the meal was served and she ate, but because he was sitting directly across from her, it was nearly impossible not to see every move he made. He was exceptionally handsome tonight, wearing a light gray suit with a pristine white cravat and shirt.

Quickly, Bridget lowered her gaze to the half-eaten food on her plate. What was she doing? Thinking how handsome he looked tonight was not a good way to get him off her mind. Instead, she should think about how handsome Collin was this evening.

She peeked at him sitting at the end of the table. He wore a dark blue jacket with matching trousers, and a white shirt and cravat. But for some reason, he just didn't stand out as much as Adrian. Collin chatted politely with Lady Margaret and Miss Sophia, who sat on either side of him, but his countenance wasn't as lively as she thought it should be.

Adrian, on the other hand, chatted briefly with his aunt, who sat on one side of him, and Felicia, who sat on the other side, but his main focus was on Bridget. His eyes sparkled with excitement every time he looked at her, making her wonder what mischievous thoughts filled his head. She chuckled softly to herself. Actually, she knew him well enough to know *exactly* what he was thinking.

As much as she tried to think of him as the deceitful scoundrel she had kissed that first day, because of his actions in saving her from the runaway horse, and his kindness when she and Priscilla were stranded with a broken vehicle, it was hard not to think of him as her hero. As often as she tried pushing those traitorous thoughts aside, the reality was that he *had* rescued her. Not just once, but twice had Adrian—not Collin—been her hero. True, Collin had been injured in both instances, but it was still his brother who came to save her.

Never had she been more frightened the day on the horse, and never had she felt more comforted as Adrian had held her close and rubbed her back while he brushed light kisses across her forehead. Sitting so near to him on the horse had felt so right. Having his arms around her, shielding her from anything harmful, had been the most perfect thing she'd experienced in such a long time.

Indeed, how could she *not* think of him as her hero?

However, she mustn't let him know that. She didn't want him to turn back into that cocksure man she first met on the estate. And if Adrian knew her heart was melting toward him, he would think he had won. That would not be a good thing at all.

When the meal was finished, the hosts invited their guests to the music room. Aunt Beatrice entertained them by playing a classical piece on the pianoforte. Bridget sat on one of the settees in the room, enjoying the familiar piece. Priscilla sat next to her, thoroughly enthralled with the old woman's playing. When Beatrice was finished, everyone applauded. She stood and curtsied, and then nudged her son Walden toward the instrument. The poor man's face turned a turnip red as he shook his head. Aunt Beatrice glared as her lips pursed.

The few sitting near Walden encouraged him to play. As soon as the man sat on the stool and positioned his fingers on the keys, Adrian stood and rubbed his forehead, moving to the back of the room. The moment Walden started playing, Bridget knew why Adrian had acted this way. She was not a rude person by nature, but it was difficult not to cringe at the man's poor playing skills.

Collin jumped up from his seat and hurried to save his cousin. When Walden peered into Collin's face, he looked vastly relieved. The men switched places, and soon Collin's talented fingers breezed across each key in a miraculous tune.

Beatrice sat next to Bridget's father and whispered something to him. He nodded and pointed toward Priscilla. There was no doubt in Bridget's mind what they were chatting about. Of all the Hartwell sisters, Prissy was the most musically inclined. Bridget played, but very little, and she liked to sing, but most people didn't like to listen when she performed. However, everyone was amazed when Prissy was the center of attention.

Suddenly, Bridget heard someone move behind her, and she inhaled a man's masculine scent of spice. Awareness buzzed in her ears and let her know exactly who was standing only inches away. She didn't dare peek over her shoulder, because she didn't want him to know she could *feel* him watching her. But oh, he smelled so nice, and those memories she wanted to keep hidden quickly resurfaced.

Inwardly, she scolded her wayward thoughts. She didn't want to think that way about him ever again, but every time he was near, her heart softened. It was difficult not to be affected by his presence.

When Collin was finished playing, everyone applauded. Aunt Beatrice stood and motioned toward Priscilla.

"Mr. Hartwell was just telling me," the older woman said loudly, "that his daughter is very talented on the pianoforte. Miss

Priscilla, would you please come and play something for us?"

Meekly, Prissy nodded and complied with the older woman's bidding. Collin stayed by the musical instrument. It was Bridget's turn to be jittery. Not because her sister didn't know how to play, but because she and Adrian were the only two in the back of the room.

Once Prissy started to play, Bridget felt Adrian's fingers brush her neck. She trembled as her racing heartbeat took off running. Warmth spread over her, stirring up feelings Adrian had awakened in her that she had tried to deny for a while now.

"Bridget," he whispered.

His hot breath stroked her skin almost as gently as a man's loving touch would.

"I need to talk to you in private," he finished in a low voice.

She inhaled a shaky breath and turned her head slightly toward him, but still didn't dare look at him. "No," she whispered over her shoulder.

She felt his fingers again, but it was more than a brush over her skin. Instead, he caressed her neck lightly. What was he doing? And *why* was he doing this? Was he purposely trying to draw attention to them? She couldn't have this. But more importantly, her father should not see what the lord's nearness was doing to her.

"It's important," Adrian said softly near her ear. "Something else has happened… to me."

Why would she care if something had happened to him? His statement was out of the ordinary, Yet she still wondered if it was just an excuse to get her alone. After all, that was the same game he had played when he asked her to meet him at the pond not too long ago.

"No," she repeated.

Priscilla finished her piece, and the applause was loud, which was normal when she played in front of a crowd. Collin enticed her to play another piece.

Adrian's touch left Bridget's neck, and she nearly sighed with relief, but seconds later, he moved around the settee and sat next to her. Inwardly, she groaned. She could not have him this close.

Bridget stiffened, and breathing had become extremely difficult. She must convince herself to relax, if only for her own sanity. If people knew why she acted this way toward Lord William, she would be labeled as one of *those* women who were easily seduced.

After a few moments without him doing anything, she relaxed. However, she should have waited, because that was when Adrian shifted in his seat and slid his arm along the back of the settee. She clenched her hands on her lap. Why was he doing this? What was *wrong* with the man?

He bent closer to her ear. "Bridget, please. Something happened earlier today, and I… I must speak to you about it."

She tossed him a scowl. "What are you implying?"

"Another accident happened."

Surprise washed over her. "What happened?"

"That is what I need to talk to you about," he continued in a whisper. "I would like your help in trying to figure out who is doing this to us."

Staring into his dreamy eyes up this close was beginning to put her in a trance, so she quickly focused back on Priscilla. Why would Adrian want to talk to her about the accident? Did he think she would be able to find the person responsible for these incidents? He knew she loved reading mystery novels, so perhaps he thought she would know how to weed out the suspects…

That was utterly ridiculous. How could she possibly help?

Oh, decisions, decisions… Yet she was curious to hear what exactly had happened to him.

Chapter Fourteen

ADRIAN SLOWLY INHALED Bridget's sweet fragrance, fighting the urge to close his eyes and smile like a child on Christmas. Her scent was already branded in his mind, and he couldn't figure out why it was so difficult to rid it from his memory. The last time his mind was constantly on a woman was when he had considered marriage. Thankfully, the young lady had changed his way of thinking, and for the better.

Strangely, though, he had thought the same way about Bridget when they first met, but over time, her personality had caught his interest, and then there was that passionate kiss they shared not long ago. He knew when she had changed his mind about her. It was when Collin had invited him to go to the Hartwell farm to be *introduced* as Lord William.

He'd been fortunate enough to overhear the conversation Bridget had with her sister. It surprised him that she was a woman who wasn't interested in Collin's money. And the more Adrian pondered on the tone of voice when asked about her feelings for Collin, how she hesitated as though she didn't know her own mind, the more thrilled Adrian had become.

He had been so wrong about her, and he really wanted her to know how wrong she was about him. He still held out hope that she wouldn't think so poorly of him, and realize that he cared for her. He enjoyed rescuing damsels in distress, especially this beauty.

At long last, Miss Priscilla finished playing, and Collin called for the servants to bring in some drinks. Their guests stood and started mingling. Bridget quickly rose to her feet, and he jumped up beside her. He touched her elbow, stopping her from leaving his side.

"Miss Hartwell," he said, loud enough that anyone nearby would hear that he was in a conversation with Bridget, but not too loud that everyone could hear, "I would really enjoy discussing your infatuation with mystery novels. I, too, enjoy reading a good mystery."

She faced him and sighed with defeat. He was grateful she finally gave in to his plea.

"What exactly do you want to discuss, Lord William?"

He found it odd how he loved hearing *Adrian* come from her mouth, instead of his first name. It didn't bother him when others called him Lord William, only Bridget. "I would like to know how you go about putting clues together as you're reading. And do you ever get to the end of the book and realize you have guessed the villain?"

She arched her eyebrow as a grin touched her face. "Are you quite serious?"

"I am."

"Mysteries and clues?" She lowered her voice. "Does this have something to do with what happened the other day while we were riding?"

"Indeed, it does."

She remained silent for a few moments, watching him through narrowed eyes. He had hoped to pique her interest, knowing how much she loved a good mystery.

"I must admit, my lord, you have made me wonder what has been happening around the estate recently." She paused. "Did it happen to just you, or were other people present?"

He shook his head. "Both my brother and I are the victims. And, of course, you were there with us while we were riding." He stepped closer and lowered his voice. "I spoke with Collin about it, and we both think that someone at the estate wants to harm us. Or... *kill* us." He whispered the last part.

She gasped. "So, perhaps I should meet with you and your brother and try to help you put clues together to can solve this mystery"—she swallowed hard—"before it's too late."

"I would like that very much, Miss Hartwell. More than you'll ever know."

Heavens, she looks so pretty this evening. Adrian sighed and smiled. She wore a light blue gown, similar to the one she had worn at the ball, but this one fit her bosom better, and showed more of her shoulders. But her hair was in a different style tonight. Her eyes were a soft blue, and her mouth was much too tempting.

He enjoyed how her gaze roamed over his face, but it was even nicer because she wasn't glaring at him. He prayed she remembered all the things they had shared in just a short time.

She licked her lips and sighed. "Are, um... you and your brother doing well?"

His heart soared. She *did* care. He wanted to touch her arm so badly, so he folded his arms to keep from following his urges. "Yes." He stepped closer. "How is your family faring?"

She smiled. "We are quite well, thank you."

"Miss Hartwell, would you and your sister like to come over to the manor tomorrow so that my brother and I can take you on a tour of the grounds? We'll be able to discuss the accidents that have been happening in more detail."

Her smile grew. "I believe I can arrange that, as long as Lord Hanover agrees."

"I'm certain he would. He enjoys your company nearly as much as I do."

Her eyes twinkled. "Then I shall ask Priscilla if she would like to come."

"Let us make it for the noon hour, and my brother and I will have a luncheon prepared."

She nodded. "That sounds lovely."

"Splendid." He stepped away from her and turned toward the others. She turned as well. Slowly, they started walking. "Do you perchance play, Miss Hartwell?" He pointed to the pianoforte.

She chuckled. "Very little. My sister is the talented one in the family."

"If you don't play, do you sing?" Adrian arched an eyebrow.

"Indeed, I do… but only to help scare away wild animals off our land."

He laughed, loving how she was able to do that to him. Not many women had a sense of humor that he enjoyed. "How very amusing you are, but I don't believe you."

"You can ask any of my sisters. They will tell you that when I try to sing, they stuff cotton in their ears."

He laughed again, and this time, some of the other guests turned their heads and looked her way. Collin also turned and looked at Adrian with a suspicious stare. The earl said something to the three women chatting with him and made his way toward Bridget. Adrian grumbled under his breath. Why couldn't Collin just let his younger brother enjoy a few moments alone with her?

When Collin reached them, she stopped and curtsied. "My lord, I must say that you are very talented on the pianoforte."

"I thank you, Miss Hartwell." Collin smiled widely. "I see my brother has been keeping you company this evening."

"Yes, he has." She glanced at Adrian. "I have been trying to convince your brother that I am not talented like my younger sister, but he doesn't believe me."

Collin folded his arms and cocked his head. "Now you have me interested as well."

"Well, I'll let you know now that I do not perform in public."

An idea popped into Adrian's head, and he grinned. "Then perhaps tomorrow, when you and your sister come over, you shall prove to us what talents you don't possess."

Collin's eyes widened. "You and Miss Priscilla are coming tomorrow?"

"Yes, dear brother. I have invited the two Hartwell sisters for a tour around our estate, and while they are here, we shall have a luncheon prepared."

"That does sound like a very entertaining afternoon." Collin's eyes gleamed. "I now find myself wishing this evening was over, only so tomorrow could get here quicker."

Satisfied with his plans, Adrian rocked back on his heels, grinning. For once, he and his brother shared the same enthusiasm. If only there was a way for Adrian to get Bridget alone tomorrow. All he needed was a few moments, and then his day would be complete.

Little by little, he was wearing down her resistance. At least she didn't appear to loathe him anymore, and because he could make her laugh, the future appeared more promising.

One way or another, he needed to show her what a good man he was. Strangely enough, the more he was with Bridget, the more he wanted to become the man she deserved.

BRIDGET COULDN'T UNDERSTAND the anticipation filling her as she hurried through her chores the next morning. In the back of her mind, she tried to think which day dress she should wear, since she only had a few that were nice enough to wear in front of titled lords. She was half tempted to borrow one of her younger sister's dresses, but then the garment would fit very snugly over the bosom. Perhaps if she could still breathe, it wouldn't matter how tightly the gown stretched across her chest.

Once she realized where her thoughts were heading, she scowled and pushed them out of her head. Why was she feeling so anxious about today's visit with the earl and Adrian, especially when she'd never gotten this excited about seeing them before?

It disturbed her greatly that her heart fluttered every time she thought of Adrian's handsome face. And that her body tingled every time he touched her. Last night was a prime example of how weak she was in his presence. But since that afternoon when he and Collin had taken her and Priscilla riding, she had seen an entirely different man.

She stared sightlessly out across the yard, while her mind filled with wonderful images. Whether she wanted to believe it or not, he had intrigued her by asking her for help in finding clues to what had been happening to him and Collin.

The question was… did Bridget really want to help them solve the mystery, or was she attending their luncheon just to see Adrian's twinkling hazel eyes that stared at her with so much emotion? Was her sole reason for going because she knew he would do all he could to stand by her, or touch her arm? She was sure he could tell his nearness made her weak in the worst way. Then again, that was probably why he continued to do that to her. He must enjoy affecting innocent women.

When Bridget made it back to the house to wash up, Priscilla was already getting ready and chattering nonstop. She didn't stop talking about the previous night and how much she had enjoyed playing the pianoforte and visiting with the earl and his aunt.

Bridget smiled. Her sister's lovely face was aglow with excitement—and maybe a touch of perspiration on her forehead—as her blue eyes sparkled. It made Bridget's heart swell with happiness to see her sister this way. Many times, during last night's party, she'd wondered if Priscilla wasn't infatuated with the earl. Collin would be blind not to notice the way Prissy watched him and blushed whenever he talked to her. He would also have to be blind not to notice that Bridget never once blushed in his presence, nor had her eyes danced with the thrill of his attention. Not like Priscilla's.

During their ride to Hanover Hall, Priscilla sat in the coach across from Bridget and nervously wrung her hands in her lap, almost to the point of digging them into her belly. It appeared that the poor girl had developed a nervous stomach. Her forehead had a slight sheen, and her cheeks were pinker than usual. Bridget had never known her sister to get worked up in this way, and she had to stop herself from laughing out loud.

"Bridget," Priscilla said, breaking the silence. "What do you think of Lord William?"

Bridget sucked in a breath. Had she read her sister's actions the wrong way? Was Prissy having these feelings for Adrian and not Collin? Or perhaps Priscilla had just noticed Bridget's attitude whenever that scoundrel was around, and she wondered about it.

Bridget swallowed, trying not to show her sister exactly how she felt about him. Until she could come to terms with her own feelings, she wasn't going to share them with anyone.

"What do I think?" Bridget laughed uncomfortably. "Pray, sister dear, am I supposed to *think* anything about him?"

Priscilla shrugged. "He is very handsome."

Bridget's heart sank a little, and she wondered if Prissy really did like Adrian more. "Yes, he is handsome, but he knows it. I don't approve of men who think they can charm women just by smiling at them." Yet she still enjoyed the way her knees grew weak when he smiled at her.

Priscilla's eyes widened. "He has already tried to charm you?"

Bridget silently groaned. She really needed to think about what she was going to say *before* saying it, especially when it was about Adrian. "We had a short conversation last night."

"Yes, I noticed." Priscilla grinned. "And from what I could see, the man is already taken with you."

Heat slowly crawled up Bridget's neck. She cursed her body's weakness. Why couldn't she stop thinking about him? And especially their kiss, and the way he had held her so tenderly while on his horse? "The man is a professional flirt and hands out his compliments too easily. But I don't believe a word that comes from his mouth."

"Why?" Prissy narrowed her gaze. "I don't understand how you are able to judge him so harshly when you have only just met him."

Bridget really should tell her sister exactly how well she knew

Adrian, but that would lead to questions she wasn't prepared to answer. "I feel I'm a good judge of character, and I think he is entirely too conceited."

Priscilla laughed. "Oh, Bridget, you are too harsh. Have you not forgotten how he raced off after you when your horse ran away? And when he brought you back, I noticed the way he held you and lifted you down. You were probably too upset over what had happened to notice, but he had a different gleam in his eyes whenever he looked your way or spoke to you."

Bridget's thoughts stalled. Had *everyone* noticed Adrian paying particular attention to her? Had Collin noticed as well? But then she realized her sister's voice seemed strained. When Bridget peered into Prissy's eyes, they appeared glassy, as though she was fighting back tears.

Oh dear. Maybe her sister *was* infatuated with Adrian and not Collin.

Jealousy had never been something Bridget experienced before, especially when it came to her younger sisters, but strangely, at this moment, the emotion clutched her chest. What were the odds Priscilla had already set her sights on the younger brother?

Bridget clasped her hands tightly together on her lap and stared out the window. The coach was slowing as they reached the front of the manor. Would she be able to remain composed in front of everyone if Prissy started flirting with Adrian?

She must. There was no other choice. Neither could she allow Adrian to think he had been able to break her heart twice since meeting him.

Chapter Fifteen

"WHY DID YOU drag Miss Hartwell into our problems?" Collin threw up his hands and paced the study like a caged animal. Each time he passed Adrian, he glared. "She is going to think our family is insane now."

"Insane? Really, Collin." Adrian shook his head. "Why would she think that? It is not our fault that these things have been happening to us. And since the servants haven't admitted to seeing anything, we need help in the matter." He leaned against the bookshelf with his arms folded across his chest. "Of all the women we have met since coming here, Miss Hartwell is the only one who will understand and actually be able to help."

Collin stopped quickly, facing Adrian. "Just because she reads mystery novels?" He shook his head. "Brother dear, I think you have lost your mind, and that is not at all reassuring."

"You weren't there when I subtly suggested she should assist us because of her knowledge." Adrian lifted his chin stubbornly. "She is interested and couldn't wait to hear more."

Collin's grumbles grew louder as he marched to the window. "You are not thinking straight." He pressed his forehead against the glass. "What if she or her sister get injured while they are here, just because they want to help us?"

Adrian grimaced. His brother's strained voice tore at his heart. Why hadn't Adrian thought of that? If something happened to Bridget, he would never forgive himself.

Groaning, he rubbed his forehead. He was a dolt… a selfish man who had only thought about having her near him just to feel the magical way his body tingled and his heartbeat knocked crazily against his ribs.

"I pray she is not the kind of woman who gossips, or we'll both be ruined," Collin continued. "What will women think if they hear someone is trying to kill us?"

Adrian looked at his brother. "Not to worry, Collin. Bridget isn't a gossipmonger. However, the two youngest Hartwell sisters are a different matter."

Collin's head snapped toward Adrian. A look of distrust was in his eyes. "*Bridget?* Why are you being so personal with her name? Has she given you permission?"

Adrian silently cursed his inability to remember those things his brother didn't know. "Don't be ridiculous. I just wanted you to know to which sister I was referring."

Sighing heavily, Collin pushed his fingers through his hair. "Adrian, one of these days, your roguish ways are going to bring me heart failure."

Adrian laughed. "*My* roguish ways? What of yours? I fear, dear brother, that if we were to compare our exploits, yours would be far greater."

Shaking his head, Collin sat on his cushioned chair as his shoulders relaxed in surrender. "No longer will I play those games. I might have lived the life of a rogue before, but coming to this manor was my new start in life. This is the very reason I'm searching for a wife."

Adrian wasn't sure he liked the forlorn tone of his brother's voice. Collin couldn't be *desperate* for a wife, could he? "Would you care to elaborate?"

"No," Collin answered gruffly.

Adrian's mind spun backward as he tried to recall all the rumors he had heard about his big brother in the past couple of years. "This wouldn't happen to be about the time you were visiting Bath with the Marquess of Kentwood, would it?"

Collin's glare darkened and his lips tightened. "Let me repeat," he said stiffly, "I do *not* want to elaborate."

Adrian had always been inquisitive, and now he was eager to know what had happened. From the rumors he'd heard a couple of years ago, Collin had ruined a woman's reputation but refused to do the gentlemanly thing and propose. But now he was turning over a new leaf and was in desperate need of a wife. How very interesting.

"Tell me one thing, Collin. Is Miss Hartwell on your list of possible wives?"

"I… I… don't know." The earl groaned as his hands covered his face. Slowly, he shook his head. "I just don't know."

Those were exactly the words Adrian wanted to hear from his brother. Now that he knew there was doubt in the earl's mind, he would help his brother by removing the lovely woman from the list. "May I ask why?"

Collin expelled a heavy breath and dropped his hands. His gaze met Adrian's.

"Miss Hartwell is a lovely woman, and I'm certain she will make some man a good wife, but she seems… Well, her personality is rather dull."

Dull? Adrian clenched his teeth. Bridget had never been dull while in his company. He found it refreshing to be around a woman who spoke her mind. It was a good thing Collin had not experienced the woman's sultry kisses, either. He would definitely think differently about her then.

"I'm surprised you feel that way, Collin. I thought you wouldn't want her because of her depleted dowry."

"No. Her family's coffers—or the lack in them—has nothing to do with my decision."

"That is very good to know." Adrian nodded. "I would hate her to be disqualified due to her family's poor circumstances."

Collin stood and moved back to the window. "I have learned a hard lesson by judging a woman because of her family's lowly circumstances. However, with Miss Hartwell, it is her drab personality that I don't find appealing."

Hope sprang inside Adrian. Now that he knew his brother wasn't interested in marrying Bridget, perhaps he had a chance of changing her thoughts toward him.

Several seconds passed in silence. Finally, Collin glanced over his shoulder at Adrian.

"Have you heard from Father recently?"

"No. I think he is still in Ireland. Why?"

"Because he urgently wants to meet with me. Yet we never seem to find a time to be in the same town at the same time."

"And that surprises you? Father has always been a busy man."

"True."

Collin returned his gaze to the window. Suddenly, he gasped. His jaw hardened and his lips thinned. His face grew redder by the second. He pointed to whatever was outside.

Adrian hurried over by him and peered into the backyard. He swept his gaze around the area but didn't see anything. "What is it?"

"There. By the oak tree. Does it look to you like a man is trying to hide?"

Once Adrian looked at the tree in the distance, he realized what his brother was staring at. But at this distance, and because of the hooded black cape the person wore, Adrian couldn't tell if it was a man or woman. But there was definitely someone trying to hide behind the wide oak tree.

Collin swore. "Tell me you saw that."

"I did," Adrian whispered as his heart hammered.

"I shall not allow this person to keep us prisoners in our own house for fear of being harmed." Collin pushed away from the window and marched toward the door. He swung it open and was ready to leave, but stopped suddenly.

The butler stood in the doorway, his hand lifted as if he'd been ready to knock. "Uh, my lords, Miss Hartwell and her sister Miss Priscilla have arrived. I showed them into the sitting room."

"Thank you, Gilbert. We'll be in momentarily." Collin glanced over his shoulder at Adrian. "Keep them entertained until I return. I'm going to get to the bottom of this trickery."

"Make sure you take a weapon." Adrian pointed to their gun cabinet.

Nodding, Collin marched to the cabinet, grabbed a pistol, and loaded it with ball and powder before leaving the room.

Adrian composed himself as his brother rushed down the corridor, heading for one of the back doors. His mind spun as he slowly stepped toward their visitors. He'd never seen his brother fire a pistol, and prayed Collin knew what he was doing.

When Adrian entered the sitting room, his gaze flew to Bridget. Her wonderful scent wafted around him. He wanted to sigh with pleasure at seeing someone so lovely in his home. But her worried expression made him pause. She sat next to her sister with her arm around Priscilla's shoulders. The younger sister's face had lost color, and moisture beaded her forehead. She had her arms against her middle as though she was in pain.

He rushed toward them and knelt beside Priscilla but peered into Bridget's pretty eyes. "What is wrong?"

"Forgive us, my lord, but my sister has suddenly become ill."

He touched Priscilla's clammy hand. "Would you like to lie down in a room?"

Priscilla's black ringlets bounced when she nodded. "If it's not… too much… trouble."

Her voice was faint and weak. Adrian knew the girl needed to lie down immediately. He glanced toward the open door of the sitting room. "Gilbert. Come here, quickly."

The shuffling of feet on the tile in the corridor was heard before the white-haired butler entered the room and bowed. "Yes, my lord?"

"We need to get Miss Priscilla to a room, posthaste. Please inform Mrs. Wendel to ready a room for her."

"As you wish, my lord." The butler hurried out.

Adrian turned back to Priscilla. "You look too weak to walk.

Can you put your arm around my neck so I can carry you?"

The younger woman nodded and slipped her arm around his shoulders. He lifted her, and Bridget assisted. His gaze met the panicked eyes of the older sister.

"Should we call for a physician?" he asked.

Bridget's attention jumped between him and her sister. The poor girl's face grew paler by the second, but her cheeks were bright red.

"Yes, I think we should." Bridget touched his shoulder and whispered, "Thank you."

He answered with a nod and proceeded to carry the sick sister up the stairs. Gilbert was just leaving one of the guest rooms, and he motioned toward it. As Adrian passed the butler, he instructed him, "Summon the physician immediately."

"Yes, my lord."

Mrs. Wendel and Bridget took Priscilla from his arms and helped her to the bed. He stood back, not knowing what to do next. He should leave, but seeing the worry on Bridget's face made him anxious to know if the younger sister would be all right.

The housekeeper poured water from a pitcher into the basin before soaking a washcloth and wringing it out. She took it to Priscilla and dabbed the cloth on her head. The older woman glanced across the bed at Bridget and frowned. "She has a high fever."

Priscilla groaned and turned her head on the pillow. Her body shook with chills. Mrs. Wendel pulled back the quilt and covered the girl. Bridget sat on the edge of the bed, holding her sister's hand.

"You're going to be all right," she said sweetly. "Lord William has sent for the physician."

Helplessness swept over him. He wanted to help in some way, but he didn't know what was proper. Being in the room with them was probably *not* proper at all. Yet he didn't want to leave.

He stepped closer to Bridget and touched her shoulder. Her big blue eyes flicked up to meet his. "What can I do?"

She gave him a sweet smile. "You have done enough by bringing her up here and sending for the doctor. I… don't know how to repay you for your kindness."

His heart leapt at her tender expression. He couldn't stop himself this time, and he caressed her soft cheek. "I do not require payment, my sweet Bridget. Getting your sister to feel better and having your gratitude is payment enough."

She reached up and removed his hand from her cheek, holding on to his fingers longer than necessary. She squeezed them affectionately before finally pulling away.

He met Mrs. Wendel's curious stare. "Is there anything I can do to help?"

"No, my lord. I have it in hand, I assure you."

That was his cue to leave. Grudgingly, he stepped toward the door, hoping that Bridget would call him back. But she didn't. Her attention was on her sickly sister.

Adrian left, closing the door behind him. He stopped at the railing on the stairs and hooked his fingers around the edge. He listened for sounds of his brother, but all he heard was the murmuring of voices between Mrs. Wendel and Bridget.

His heart softened as he recalled how her pretty eyes had shone with appreciation just now. Although he felt helpless because he had no idea what to do for Priscilla, happiness leapt inside him. Bridget was slowly forgiving him.

He hadn't thought of any other woman since the adorable Hartwell sister had entered his life. As much as he felt he knew her well enough, he still wanted to learn more. He wanted to make friends with her father and other sisters, and he wanted to know what Bridget did every second of the day. He especially wanted to know if he was on her mind too, or if she still aspired to become the Countess of Hanover.

The click of the door closing behind him made him swing around to see who had come out. Bridget walked toward him.

The tender look in her eyes made his pulse quicken.

She stopped in front of him and grasped one of his hands. His heart jumped to his throat. He lifted her hand to his mouth and brushed a kiss across her knuckles.

"Adrian, I want to thank you again for allowing my sister to lie down. But Mrs. Wendel says Prissy's fever is getting higher. I fear we might not be able to move her when it's time to leave."

"There's absolutely no need to do that. She shall stay here until she is well." He kissed her knuckles again, slower this time, loving the softness of her skin against his lips.

"I thank you, Adrian," she whispered. "But I should send word to my father."

"Allow me," he said quickly, wanting to do anything that would make her happy.

She nodded, her smile growing. "You don't know how much I appreciate your help."

She reached her other hand up and cupped the side of his face. He hitched a breath. She had made the first move to touch him, and not only that, but the look in her tantalizing gaze was one he had not seen before. Warmth spread through him, and his heart swelled.

He wanted to take her in his arms and show her with his lips how much this moment meant to him. But any one of his servants could walk by and see them kissing. Even Collin could catch them in an intimate embrace.

Expelling his breath slowly, Adrian covered her hand that still rested on his cheek, turned his head, and placed a kiss on her palm. Her throat jumped with what must have been a hard swallow, and the pulse at her neck beat quickly.

"What can I do for you, my lovely Bridget? Name it and it's yours."

Her shoulders relaxed. "Just send a note to my father. That is all I need at the moment."

Nodding, he took both of her hands and kissed each one before releasing her and heading for the stairs. Happiness filled him, giving him hope for a brighter future. At least for now, he felt she would be easier to convince that he wasn't a horrid scoundrel after all.

Chapter Sixteen

BRIDGET WAS MENTALLY and physically exhausted. The doctor had examined Priscilla and thought that she might have typhus—which, thankfully, wasn't contagious. He had noticed a bug bite on the back of her arm and decided that was how she'd become infected. Unfortunately, he wasn't certain how long she would be sick, and he even suggested that typhus could take Priscilla's life. Bridget knew that prayers were the only thing to heal her sister.

Her father and sisters had visited earlier today but left within a few hours. Adrian insisted that Bridget stay by her sister's side, and he let her father know they were welcome to stay for as long as they needed.

Smiling, she realized Adrian had changed drastically. She approved of the man he had proven himself to be. Bridget moved her fork around her plate, cherishing the silence in the dining room as she ate. Mealtimes at her house were rarely quiet. But being alone also made her uncomfortable. Not often did she eat by herself. In fact, she wished she could have taken her meal in the guestroom where Mrs. Wendel had placed her, next to Priscilla's room.

The food smelled heavenly, but as Bridget ate, her mind wasn't on the taste. Her thoughts had moved away from her sickly sister and were completely occupied with one man—

Adrian.

It was different thinking about him in a new light. She liked the changes in him. Or… was it she who had changed? Had he been caring and selfless all this time and she hadn't noticed?

No, he was the one different now. When they first met, he would have never thought of others first.

The last few times they had been together, she'd felt her feelings toward him softening. And when she talked to him by the stair railing, it was all she could do not to throw her arms around him and kiss him soundly on the mouth. When he had brushed his lips across her knuckles, shivers of delight had rippled through her and made her weak in the knees.

What she wasn't certain about was whether he had *really* changed—or had those things she'd witnessed in the past few days been just an act for her sake? If he *had* become the kind and selfless man she wanted, it would be very easy to fall in love with him, especially since she had been fighting those feelings since their first kiss.

"Bridget."

Hearing her name in his deep voice brought her out of her thoughts. She looked up from her plate. He entered the dining room and walked toward her.

"How are you faring, my sweet Bridget?"

She blew out a tired breath. "If I wasn't so exhausted, I would be able to tell you how I was faring."

He sat beside her and touched her hand. "Caring for a sick relative takes its toll on us, that is certain."

"You have taken care of someone who was ill?"

He nodded. "My mother." He shrugged. "I suppose I wasn't the only one who cared for her, but I was only fourteen at the time, and worrying endlessly about her was exhausting. I hadn't dared even leave the manor for fear she would die before I had a chance to say goodbye."

"Did she… die?"

He nodded. "She left this world, unfortunately."

"I'm very sorry for your loss. I must admit, I'm extremely worried about my sister. I've never seen her so sick. And the doctor doesn't give much hope of a quick recovery, especially if she goes over three days of having a high fever."

He gently squeezed her hand. "Then we must not let the fever go that long."

"Your servants have been most attentive. I shall never be able to repay your kindness, my lord."

"Think nothing of it, my sweet Bridget. I'm just relieved my servants are so quick to assist."

She didn't have the energy—or the heart—to pull away. The warmth from his hand merged with hers, creating a sense of comfort. If she didn't think she would fall asleep, she would happily stare into his beautiful hazel eyes all night.

Using her other hand, she sipped her wine, mainly to bring moisture back into her dry mouth and throat. "Adrian, I must apologize for our afternoon plans being ruined."

"There is no need to apologize. We can always give you a tour when your sister is feeling better."

She placed her glass of wine back on the table and turned toward him. "I am, however, still intrigued about what has been happening to you and your brother."

His eyes widened, and he chuckled. "I had actually forgotten about that."

"Will you tell me?"

"Are you sure you want to hear it? As tired as you are, you might doze off on me."

She laughed. "I promise to stay alert."

He glanced at her plate of half-eaten food. "Are you finished? Perhaps we could adjourn to the sitting room."

"Yes, I'm finished."

They both stood at the same time, and he offered his arm. As she slipped her hand around his elbow, she fought the urge to cuddle against him. They walked toward the sitting room, and she realized how hard it was not to stare at his handsome profile.

He moved with such grace and elegance that she felt privileged to be the woman beside him. Indeed, he wasn't the scoundrel she first thought, but instead, a true gentleman.

They reached the sitting room and sat together on the settee. Thankfully, he left the door open, but she almost wished he would close it. Then again, her mind was tired, and she knew it would be hard to fight the impulses she received every time they were alone.

His shoulders relaxed. "Well, I need not tell you about Collin getting shot at because you were there—however, more things have been happening to him, as well as to me."

"Tell me."

He explained to her about the saddle girth being cut, the stairs' railing being broken, the plant falling over the banister, and lastly the person wearing a black cape who had been hiding behind the oak tree in the yard. She tried hard to listen to what he was saying, but the hypnotic sound of his deep voice, mixed with his entrancing eyes, had put her under a spell. She couldn't stop admiring his masculine face. It was as if a famous sculptor had chiseled every detail, from Adrian's high forehead to his straight nose and high cheekbones, down to those tempting lips that made her stomach flutter just from thinking about them pressed against her mouth. His broad shoulders and broad chest tapered to slim hips. She had been in his embrace enough times to know how muscular he was.

When he paused, she quickly focused on what he had been telling her. "What did your brother find when he went outside to search for the person in the black cape?"

"Collin didn't find anything. It was as if the person just disappeared."

"Did you hear nothing after your brother left the manor? Any footsteps or doors closing that might announce a servant coming inside?"

"Nothing." His expression softened. "But then, my mind wasn't on trying to detect footsteps or the doors closing. It was preoccupied with the very lovely and intriguing woman who had come to visit."

Her cheeks warmed from his confession that he had been thinking about her, too. "Were you perhaps cursing me in your mind because I had come at the wrong time?"

"On the contrary, my lovely Bridget." He stretched his arm across the back of the settee behind her, which moved him closer to her. "My recollection is that I had been, in fact, thinking about your smell."

Inwardly, she groaned. She smelled like the farm again, she just knew it. "My *smell*?"

"Yes, your exhilarating lilac scent that has been on my mind ever since we were in the pantry."

He leaned closer as his face fell to her neck. She held her breath as her heartbeat sped out of control. He brushed away the ringlets resting on her shoulder with his fingers, and his knuckles touched her neck. Pleasurable shivers ran through her, and she couldn't stop them. She didn't want to.

He inhaled deeply before very slowly pulling away. When his eyes met hers, she recognized the look of passion she had witnessed on his face so many times since meeting him. But whether it was because she was so tired or if it was because she really wanted him to kiss her, she didn't know… as long as a kiss followed shortly.

"Your scent is unforgettable," he whispered. "I smell you everywhere, it seems. Even in my dreams."

Her mouth grew dry again, and she licked her lips. His gaze dropped to her mouth. She was breathing so heavily she might just put herself to sleep. Yet her body and mind were awakening in ways she never imagined, and she wanted to taste his sweet kiss one more time. But was she ready for it? Kissing Adrian would make her feel things she had hoped to forget.

"Wha… what happened next?" she said in a shaky voice.

"What *happens* next?" The corner of his mouth stretched higher than the other. "Well, my love, I would think a kiss would be what would happen next. Don't you?"

Oh, heavens! Had he truly referred to her as *my love*? Her heartbeat accelerated even more, but she mustn't show him how much those two little words meant. Not until she could figure out her own feelings.

Returning to the conversation, she realized he was taking her words and twisting them again. "No, I mean, with your brother and the unknown person by the tree?"

"You think I should kiss the unknown person?" He laughed loudly and leaned closer. "My sweet Bridget, that is simply out of the question. Besides, I would rather kiss the lovely woman I cannot stop staring at. I would rather have you constantly on my mind. It's more pleasurable that way."

"But what if… if…" She swallowed the cotton that had somehow formed in her throat again. "What if your brother comes in? How do we explain it to him?"

He moved his fingers to her forehead and then trailed them across and down the side of her face, going further to her neck. She loved his touch but was worried that if she didn't stop him now, she might never want him to stop.

"Tell me honestly, Bridget," he said softly, "how do you feel about my brother? Are you still hoping he will propose?"

"I… I…"

"Do you love him, Bridget?" He moved his hand up, cupping the side of her face. "Because if you do, I shall back away and not get between you and Collin."

Her mind felt dizzy, but it was because he was forcing her to decide. Could she admit that she'd never had feelings for Collin? Yet if she told Adrian that, she would have to confess that he was the man who'd filled her thoughts, even when she disliked him.

"You… would do that?" she asked.

He nodded. "Just tell me that you are in love with my brother, and I shall stop trying to win your affections."

Her heart twisted. What was wrong with her? Why couldn't she tell him? Perhaps she was still afraid he would break her heart.

ADRIAN SAW THE hesitation on her face, but she couldn't possibly love Collin. When Bridget and his brother were together, it was quite obvious to Adrian that she was uncomfortable around Collin. Adrian knew her body language by now, and if she told him she loved Collin, he would know it was untrue.

"But," he said quickly, before she could answer his question, "I want you to remember something."

"What?"

"I want you to remember this." He pulled her face toward him and captured her mouth. She inhaled sharply, but seconds later, she sighed and melted against him. He took her into his arms and kissed her meaningfully—not the urgent way they had kissed in the pantry. Now, he wanted this kiss to make her feel something else. He wanted her to experience the yearning emotions that were shooting through him, and he prayed she would feel the same way.

Her arms slid around his shoulders, and he pulled her against him. Tilting his head, he deepened the kiss, and it thrilled him when she responded eagerly. Her fingers moved to his hair, stroking the strands before she delved deeper, touching his scalp. Her tender caress made him sigh with pleasure.

Suddenly, she cupped his face and broke the kiss. He couldn't catch his breath as he stared into her lovely eyes.

"Adrian?"

"Yes, love?"

"I… don't have any feelings for your brother. I never did."

Groaning with happiness, he gathered her against him once more, turning the kiss wild. He heard Collin's voice coming from the corridor, asking the butler where Adrian was. Grumbling, he pulled away and quickly stood to move toward the window. He inhaled deeply, trying to compose himself under the desire flaming inside him. All Collin would have to do was take one look at Adrian's expression to know what had just happened.

In the reflection of the window, he saw Bridget smoothing out the wrinkles on her dress before patting her hair in place. Her cheeks were bright red, and he prayed she would be able to control her embarrassment. Indeed, a blind man would be able to feel the heat sparking between Bridget and himself.

Collin's heavy footsteps announced him as he entered the room. "William, I—" He hitched a breath. "Miss Hartwell, I didn't know you were here."

Adrian turned just as his brother sat next to the flustered woman on the settee. Collin took Bridget's hand, and as he stared into her face, his expression told of his worry. Trying not to grin, Adrian bit the inside of his cheek. If Collin had been paying any attention, he would know. Perhaps it was the eldest brother who thought only of himself instead of the younger.

"How is your sister?" Collin asked.

"Her fever is still quite high, I'm afraid. But your physician promises to keep a close eye on her."

"And he will. He is the best doctor around."

She gave Collin a small smile. "I do appreciate your kindness, and Lord William's, of course."

"Think nothing of it."

Collin patted her hand, and Adrian noticed she subtly pulled away. Her attention moved to him, and he wanted to shout with victory. Indeed, he had won the lovely maiden, not the brother with the title. This proved to Adrian that she was not the farthing-filching woman he had originally wanted to keep away from his family.

"Lord William was telling me about the accidents that have been happening to the two of you lately." She looked back at Collin. "And he mentioned that you saw someone outside earlier today just as my sister and I arrived. I hope you're not too uncomfortable sharing that with me."

Collin's face hardened as he threw Adrian a glare. "My brother should learn when to keep his mouth shut."

"Oh, no, my lord." She touched Collin's arm until he looked at her, and then she withdrew. "I'm eager to help you figure out what has been happening around the manor."

Shrugging, Collin leaned back in the settee. "I fear it's worse than I suspected… as if someone is trying to make us go insane with worry."

She tilted her head and narrowed her gaze. "Why would you think that?"

Collin exchanged glances with Adrian. "Because nothing makes sense."

"What doesn't make sense?" she asked.

Collin shifted in his seat, clearly uncomfortable with the topic. Adrian knew it was because his brother didn't want people to know what was happening for fear that they would become injured as well.

"Miss Hartwell," Adrian said, moving to the chair next to her, "we believe someone is purposely trying to harm us."

"Someone here in the manor?" Bridget's eyebrows lifted. "But when I talked with your maid the day the wheel broke from my buggy, she said that the staff are all very devoted to you and the earl."

"We believe so. After all, when the pot fell from the banister, only someone in the house could have done that."

She shrugged. "Or a servant was paid to help the true villain."

Adrian sucked in a quick breath and exchanged a surprised glance with his brother. When Adrian returned his attention to Bridget, he smiled. "I suppose that is a possibility. That deduction is utterly brilliant."

Her cheeks bloomed with color. "I'm not sure about it being brilliant, but tell me, have there been any threatening notes to either of you?"

Adrian shook his head. He only suspected his brother gave the same response, because Adrian couldn't look at anything else in the room right now. Bridget Hartwell's beauty and intellect literally took his breath away.

"Why do you ask, my dear?"

"I recall when the last people who lived here had to move. It was done so quickly and in the middle of the night."

"Why is that, I wonder?" Collin asked, leaning closer to her on the settee.

She briefly glanced at the man next to her before returning her attention to Adrian. "Their unwed daughter was in the family way, and they didn't want to create a scandal."

Adrian hitched a breath, shocked that Bridget would know about that delicate rumor, especially when he remembered that she had scolded her sisters for gossiping. But the tale intrigued him, nonetheless.

"However," Bridget continued, "the scandal broadens. You see, the unwed girl's older brother was a gambler, and before they moved, my father learned of some men who had come to the manor and met with Lord Caldwell, and, well… the ruffians scuffed him up pretty badly." She paused briefly. "It makes me wonder if these men don't know that the Caldwell family have moved, and they are creating these accidents for the sole purpose of trying to exact revenge on Lord Caldwell, who reportedly gambled away his inheritance."

Adrian realized their father must have known about the scandal. Why else would he had purchased the manor so cheaply?

"That makes sense." Collin nodded. "After all, Adrian and I have not upset anyone in our lives—that we know about, anyway—especially since moving here. I cannot see anyone wanting to harm or kill us. I believe it's worth bringing the constable in on this to have him check out a few leads."

"Indeed," Bridget said. "I think the constable would recall the incident when those men were fighting with Lord Caldwell."

Collin jumped to his feet, appearing eager to summon the man of the law, but then he looked to the window and frowned.

"I suppose I'll have to talk to the constable tomorrow. I hadn't realized how late it was."

Bridget met Adrian's stare and shrugged. There were no

words between them, but he still knew what she was thinking. He, too, wished his brother could talk to the constable tonight so that Adrian and Bridget could continue their passionate kiss.

Sighing, she smoothed her hands on her dress and stood. "Since it's late, I think I shall retire for the night. I've had a very long and exhausting day."

Adrian locked gazes with her and smiled as he bowed slightly. "Have a good rest, Miss Hartwell."

"I thank you, Lord William."

Collin threw a glance over his shoulder. "Good night, Miss Hartwell."

"To you as well, Lord Hanover."

Adrian watched her leave the room, and just before she turned, she peeked back inside. Her gaze went directly to him, and she smiled widely. His heart soared. The feelings he had for her confused him, yet at the same time, he never wanted them to stop.

He listened as her footsteps gradually disappeared. A deep sigh escaped him, and he sat back in his chair. The days were not long enough for all the time he wanted to spend with her, talking, gazing into each other's eyes, and kissing her passionately.

"My dear brother," Collin said, "might I ask what your intentions are with Miss Hartwell?"

Chapter Seventeen

ADRIAN SNAPPED TO a sitting position and jerked his head around to look at his brother. "Pardon me?"

Collin rolled his eyes and moved to the side bar to pour himself a brandy. "You heard me, so stop acting as though you don't know what I'm talking about."

"What makes you think I have any inten—"

"It's obvious that you are in love with her." Collin arched an eyebrow. "And I must say, it's quite shocking to see that you have finally given your heart away."

Chuckling uncomfortably, Adrian shook his head. "Love? Oh, I think not, Collin."

"Then answer this for me, if you will." Collin paused and narrowed his gaze on Adrian as he took another sip. "Is she on your mind constantly, day and night? When you think of her, do you find yourself grinning like a fool?"

Slowly, Adrian nodded. "It sounds as though you understand my feelings well, dear brother. That tells me you have felt this way before."

"Yes, I have had similar emotions." Collin finished his drink in one gulp.

Confusion filled Adrian. "Then why are you not married to the fortunate woman?"

Collin laughed forcefully and moved back to the liquor tray.

"Because I was the biggest fool of them all, and I waited too long to declare my love." He sighed. "By the time I knew my own feelings, she was engaged to another man."

"And you let that keep you from confessing your love?" Adrian moved out of his chair and went to stand by his brother. "You are the Earl of Hanover. You could have any woman you want."

"No, brother. Not any woman. This woman was the daughter of an impoverished baron. Although they lived in a large cottage, it was in need of major repairs. In the *ton*'s eyes, the baron and his family were no less than farmers, similar to Miss Hartwell's. My best friend was caught in a compromising position with the woman, and her father forced Kentwood to wed her. I wouldn't have been able to stop it even if I wanted."

"Kentwood? Are you referring to Lloyd Talbot, our mother's cousin?"

"Yes, that was who ended up with the woman who held my heart."

Adrian blew out a gust of air, understanding what his brother was saying. "Forgive me, but I hadn't realized—"

"How could you?" Collin shrugged. "This happened a year ago when I traveled to Bath with Kentwood. We met the young miss and her family, but I judged her harshly. When I realized how I felt about Cassandra, it was too late." A smile slowly crossed his face. "She was a stubborn woman, yet she made me laugh. She was well liked by those around her." He sighed again. "I'm sure she has made Kentwood a wonderful wife."

"Did you attend their wedding?"

"No. I couldn't bring myself to watch it happen. I left, and I haven't seen or spoken to Lloyd since."

"Is that why you went traveling the world after you were in Bath?"

Collin nodded. "I was trying to get rid of my feelings for her."

"Did it work?"

"Not exactly." Collin set his empty glass down on the tray before turning toward Adrian. "What I'm trying to tell you, dear brother, is that if you're in love with Miss Hartwell, you need to let her know. Don't hide your feelings, because you never know what tomorrow will bring. One never knows when love will be taken from us."

Adrian patted Collin's shoulder. This was the first time he'd felt so close to his brother. "Then I won't make your mistake."

"Splendid. Tell her as soon as you can… however, given the time of night, I suggest you wait for the morning."

Adrian laughed loudly. "I'm not sure if I can, but I shall try."

Collin gave him that big-brother scowl. "Don't turn this into a scandal. Quick marriages ruin the woman's family name."

"I'm aware of that."

Chuckling, Adrian left the room and made his way toward his bedchambers. He really should wait until morning, but with his heart so full of this odd, tender emotion, would he be able to hold off from seeing her until then?

He highly doubted it.

BRIDGET SLEPT LIKE the dead for a few hours, but then became wide awake. She jumped out of bed, shrugged into her dressing gown, and slipped her feet into slippers before hurrying out of the room. She quietly entered the guest room where Priscilla was sleeping and tiptoed to the bed. A lamp on the bedside table was turned low. The odor of sickness filled the room. Priscilla was still looking pale and clammy, and her breaths were ragged and deep. Beads of moisture coated her forehead, and her pillow was slightly damp.

She knew Mrs. Wendel had been checking on her, but Bridget wondered if she should stay and keep watch over her dear sister.

"Oh, Prissy." She sat on the edge of the bed and held her sister's hot hand. "You need to pull through this," she whispered. "I can't lose my favorite sister and my best friend."

Closing her eyes, Bridget said a silent prayer, begging the Lord to heal her most beloved sibling. As she finished with the prayer, she wiped the tears from her eyes and peered back at Priscilla.

Bridget moved to the washbasin and placed the dry hand cloth in the cool water. Once she had drenched it and wrung it out, she took it back to her sister and lightly dabbed her forehead. A small moan came, but Prissy didn't open her eyes.

Soft footsteps and the click of the door opening alerted Bridget to someone entering. She looked over her shoulder. Adrian stood just inside the room, looking very casual, and extremely handsome. He wore only his trousers, shirt, and vest, and without his cravat, she could see his muscular neck and a little of his chest, making his shoulders appear wider. His hair wasn't as perfect as usual, but it made him even more attractive. It was all she could do not to sigh aloud.

Seeing him this way reminded her of the dreams she'd had last night. It was just the two of them, holding each other, talking… and yes, definitely kissing. Suddenly, her mouth became parched, and she licked her lips.

"How is your sister faring?" he whispered, leaving the door open as he moved closer to the bed.

Bridget looked away from him, only because he was making her breathless. "I don't see a difference in her health at all."

He stopped beside her and rested his warm hand on her shoulder. Awareness buzzed through her, making her remember she was still wearing her nightclothes. This was certainly very inappropriate. However, she didn't have the will to beg him to leave. After all, this was his home. Not only that, but his presence also comforted her greatly.

"Don't give up hope," he said. "Your sister is strong. I'm sure she will pull through." He gently squeezed her shoulder.

She lifted her hand and covered his. His thumb stroked her knuckles. "Oh, Adrian. I pray you're right. I don't know what I would do if I lost her."

"Shhh..." He bent and kissed the top of her head. "There will be no more negative thoughts. From now on, only people with positive attitudes will be in this room. I believe that your sister will feel our energy and her illness will leave her body."

Tears burned her eyes and her heart melted. "Thank you, Adrian. You are wonderful."

She hesitated to look at him, yet she needed to see his reassuring smile and his comforting gaze. She turned her head toward him. Just as she had figured, his smile melted her heart.

"Do you want me to get you anything? Are you hungry?"

"No, Adrian. I'm fine."

"Do you wish me to fetch Mrs. Wendel?"

Bridget nodded. "I think the sheets and pillowcase need to be changed. Because of Prissy's fever, they have grown damp."

"Then I shall get her now."

He turned, but she grasped his hand to stop him from leaving. His gaze locked with hers again.

"Thank you, Adrian. I... I don't know what I would do without you."

Although the light in the room wasn't very bright, she noticed the twinkle in his amazing eyes. Seconds later, he bent and kissed her on the mouth, but it was very brief. He withdrew, but not very far.

"Bridget, I will be here for you. Always."

Tears continued to fill her eyes, even as he turned and left the room. Her heart hammered so fast that she feared she would be the one lying on death's bed soon. She needed to tell him how she felt. If she hid it any longer, her courage would be gone.

She jumped off the bed and ran after him. "Adrian, wait."

He stopped in front of the room, and she rushed to him. His eyes widened as he opened his arms for her. The moment she pressed against him, he wound them tightly around her.

"What is it, my love?"

She sighed heavily, treasuring the way his voice sounded when he said that to her. "Adrian, I... I must tell you something."

"What is it?" His fingers brushed a lock of hair off her forehead.

She opened her mouth to speak, but the words weren't forthcoming. Never had she told a man she loved him, and she wasn't sure if she could do it now.

She laughed lightly. "I cannot believe how tongue-tied I am. I have wanted to tell you something since last night, but…"

"Your tongue is not working properly?" He grinned as one of his eyebrows arched and his gaze dropped to her mouth. "Then pray, allow me to fix that for you."

He bent his head and captured her mouth. Sighing in pleasure, she slid her arms around his neck. Immediately, the kiss grew urgent and very passionate. Her heart felt as if it had grown at least three sizes larger, and she knew she would have no difficulty telling him how she felt now. When she was done kissing him, anyway.

As they kissed, his hands moved to her hair and he threaded his fingers through her long curls. He gently held her head between his hands and deepened the kiss even more. She slid her hands down his wide chest and clutched his vest.

"Bridget, my love." His mouth moved from her lips and down her throat. "I've been thinking about doing this to you all night long."

She opened her eyes to look at him. "And I have had the same yearnings for you."

"I don't know how it happened, but…" He lifted his head and gazed into her eyes. "But I have fallen madly in love with you."

She moaned in happiness. "I have tried to fight my feelings, but I cannot. You hold my heart, and I want you to have it. Always."

He slipped his arms around her waist and pulled her closer. This time when his mouth covered hers, the kiss was so very tender, so very meaningful, and she could have cried with joy.

They kissed for a few minutes longer before he pulled away again. This time, he dropped his head on her shoulder and breathed on her neck. Shivers cascaded over her, making her snuggle against him. She couldn't get enough of his nearness, even though this was very improper.

"Bridget, my love," he said in a deep voice, "my brother knows how I feel about you."

She held her breath. "He does?"

"And he urged me to tell you how I feel."

Relief poured through her, and she smiled. "I'm so happy he understands."

"As am I." He pulled back and looked at her. "But that wouldn't have stopped me. I was falling for you from the first time I saw you in my yard scolding your sisters for trespassing."

She laughed. "And I was having feelings for you when you tried to convince me I was a farthing-filching woman."

"I know you're not now."

She tilted her head. "You do?"

"I overheard you tell your sister the day Collin brought me to your house and introduced me as his brother, but"—he shook his head—"it wouldn't have mattered to me even if you were. I was attracted to you, and I enjoy being in your company. I love how you make me laugh."

"And I love how you laugh with me."

He stroked her back as she rested her face on his chest, pressing her cheek intimately against the skin at his neck where his shirt was open.

"Bridget, my love. You do know what comes next, correct?"

She smiled and snuggled closer. "Are you referring to the talk you are going to have with my father?"

His chest shook with a silent laugh. "Indeed. That is exactly what I'm referring to."

"As much as I want you to talk to him today, will you wait until Priscilla recovers?"

Adrian kissed the top of her head. "Of course I will. I'll do anything to make you happy."

She turned her head slightly and kissed his throat. "Well, for now, I suppose"—she kissed his neck again, letting her lips linger a moment longer on his hot skin—"we should find somewhere private, and..."

"Bridget?"

Her sister's voice jerked Bridget away from Adrian. She looked up at him, and his eyes were wide with surprise. She gasped and rushed into the room.

Priscilla's eyes were open, and she struggled to smile when she saw Bridget.

"You're awake!" Bridget dropped on the edge of the bed and touched her sister's hand. It didn't feel as hot. She checked her forehead, and that too felt slightly cooler. She looked over her shoulder. Adrian stood at the doorway. "Adrian, go wake up Mrs. Wendel. I believe my sister is starting to recover."

His smile widened before he turned and ran down the corridor. When Bridget looked back at her sister, Prissy's eyebrow was arched.

"Is there something I need to know about you and Lord William," Priscilla rasped, "and especially why you call him Adrian?"

Bridget laughed. "Yes, but let's wait until Mrs. Wendel checks on you. Then I'll be ready to tell you all of the juicy details of my love life."

Prissy gave her a lazy smile. "And in the meantime... I'm hungry."

Chapter Eighteen

BRIDGET HOOKED HER arm around Adrian's as they strolled outside through the gardens. There was a light wind in the air, which brought with it a slight chill, but the early evening's backdrop set the romantic mood, and she couldn't pass up the opportunity to be alone with him. Knowing that Priscilla was on her way to a full recovery helped relieve Bridget's mind. It had been three days since her sister's fever had broken, and Adrian had invited her family over for supper, since his own father had unexpectedly arrived to visit. Before the meal was ready, Bridget and Adrian took her father aside so that Adrian could ask permission to marry her. It had been many years since she had seen her father that ecstatic.

During the meal, they announced their engagement, and everyone rejoiced. Bridget was happy to see Adrian's father looking so proud… and shocked. After all, she was a mere country girl and didn't come from old money or a titled lineage.

But then there was another surprise—both sad and happy. Adrian's father announced that Collin had inherited the title of marquess. His distant cousin, Lloyd Talbot, Marquess of Kentwood, had passed away. Bridget could tell Collin wasn't sure how to handle this news. But what was even more startling was that Adrian had seemed just as perplexed.

"Are you cold, my love?" Adrian asked.

"No. I have my cape to keep me warm."

He rubbed her arm. "Let me know if you become chilled. I know an excellent way to keep us both warm."

Grinning, she pressed the side of her head against Adrian's arm. Since she had confessed her love to him, she felt as though she walked on clouds. Not even her dreams were this good.

"I believe, my sweet man, that you brought me out here knowing a storm was brewing, so you could offer me the warmth of your body."

"Is that so bad?" He chuckled.

"Not at all. In fact, I encourage that kind of behavior in my soon-to-be husband."

"You know me well, and you will know I'm only happy to comply."

They walked slowly. She was so very happy to be with him, and not have to worry about causing a scandal because they were alone.

"You've been awfully quiet this evening," Bridget said. "Ever since your father announced the death of your cousin, both you and Collin haven't been very talkative."

His smile disappeared, and he nodded. "Collin told me what happened a year ago when he and Lloyd went to Bath. Believe it or not, my brother had given his heart to a woman. Unfortunately, she was compromised by Lloyd, and they were forced to wed."

She gasped. "But… your cousin died."

"Yes, in a boating accident with several of his drunken friends."

"But Adrian… the woman Collin gave his heart to is now a *widow*. And he is now the marquess."

Adrian stopped and faced her. She slid her arms around his waist as his arms encircled her shoulders.

"Exactly."

"What do you think your brother will do?"

"That, my darling Bridget, is a very good question, which I'm sure my brother is contemplating as we speak. However, I realize that is his decision to make, so I must stop worrying about him."

She smiled. "You're just being kindhearted."

He chuckled and held her tighter. "Indeed, but if you knew the past I had with my brother, you would find that most comical."

Laughing, she shook her head and turned, hooking her arm around his again to continue their stroll. "I'm happy to know both of you have matured since then. I'm not certain I would be able to tolerate that kind of behavior between my husband and brother-in-law."

He sighed heavily. "But now, I wonder if Collin has doubts about your sister."

Just as her mind gathered the information and processed it, her feet slowed the pace. "What do you mean?"

Adrian shrugged. "I noticed that Collin has been enjoying himself with Priscilla, and, well, I wondered if he was developing feelings for her."

"I had actually thought Priscilla had been in love with you, but now that I think about it, you are correct. All this time, she kept asking how I felt about marrying the earl, and I couldn't answer her because I was falling in love with you. But now, I see that she was referring to Collin."

"Yes, but now... Well, I believe Collin will consider Lady Kentwood in the running once again. He never stopped loving the woman."

"I hope, for Priscilla's sake, that Collin really thinks about this. Although he may be interested in my sister, he does not look at her as though he is in love." Bridget smiled and touched his cheek. "His expression is nowhere near the way you look at me."

"I confess, I lose myself whenever you are around."

Her heart skipped wildly. "I know the feeling well."

He leaned down to kiss her, but a nearby rustling noise distracted him. Adrian swung around, and Bridget tried to peer through the thickening shadows to see who else was outside. He took her hand and crept toward the corner of the house, and then stopped. Together, they cautiously peeked around the corner.

Someone was out there, and whoever it was had set up a ladder against the large oak tree a few feet from the house. Although Bridget couldn't see who it was, the person was wearing a black cape.

She gasped, and Adrian's quick intake of breath soon followed. He pulled her flat against the wall of the house, keeping out of sight of the intruder by the tree.

"I believe we have found the person Collin saw a few days ago who was trying to hide," she whispered.

He nodded. "Yes, I think you are correct, my love. But we must tread carefully. I won't allow him to harm you. Now that I realize how important you are to me, I must protect you at all costs."

"My darling man, have you forgotten how stubborn I am? If we work together, we can overpower this person and catch him."

She peered around the corner again, watching closely. Their threat held an axe in one hand and slowly climbed the ladder. Once he reached the top, the mystery villain carefully stepped onto a branch. Then the unknown person climbed to a higher branch and slid toward a window.

Adrian's arms were wrapped around her middle as he stood behind her, peering over her shoulder. His warm breath brushed against her cheek.

"That is one of the windows to my bedchamber," Adrian whispered. "I wonder what he is planning."

"Is it a man?" she asked. "It almost looks like it could be a woman, because whoever it is, they are thin and not very tall."

"Very true."

Several minutes passed in silence as they continued to watch the unknown person slowly chop at the branch closest to Adrian's window. Just before the branch was chopped off completely, the person moved to another branch and started chopping on that. The wind caught the person's hood and pulled it off. It was a man with thinning hair. He quickly pulled the hood back over his head.

Adrian swore softly as he pulled her back around the house and pressed her up against the wall. When she looked into his shadowed face, she could see his tight lips. He wrapped an arm around her shoulders, bringing her closer as he bent his mouth to her ear.

"It's Cousin Walden."

She sucked in a quick breath. "Are you sure?"

"I would recognize that balding head anywhere."

"What is he doing with those branches?"

He withdrew just enough to look into her eyes. "My guess is he is weakening the branches so they will easily break when the wind becomes stronger as it ushers in the storm tonight."

"But *why* would he want to do that? If you're in your room during that time, you could get hurt."

His eyes widened and his jaw hardened. "Exactly."

"But… why would he want to harm his own cousins?"

Adrian nodded slowly. "Everything makes sense now. These so-called accidents didn't start happening until after he and Aunt Beatrice arrived." He paused briefly. "Don't you see, my love? If Collin dies, the earldom will go to me, and if something happens to me and I die, the title will go to none other than my cousin, Walden."

She gasped and quickly covered her mouth. "Oh dear. We cannot let that happen."

He caressed her cheek. "Now that we know, we won't allow him win. But now we have to think of a way to get him to confess to everything he has been doing."

Silence stretched between them for a few minutes as her mind whirled with possibilities. All she could think of at this moment were the many pranks her sisters had pulled over the years, and how she had always been able to retaliate with something even better.

Suddenly, an idea struck her, and she grasped Adrian's coat. "I have an idea."

"You do?"

"Yes." She grinned. "But we shall need a slingshot."

His chest shook with silent laughter. "I have one."

"Go get it."

He kissed her on the mouth. "I can't wait to see what you have planned."

IT DIDN'T TAKE long for Adrian to find his slingshot. Bridget took it and found several small rocks around the edge of the manor. Thankfully, his foolish cousin was still up in the tree, chopping at more branches. The wind had picked up, so Adrian was certain Walden would want to end his chopping soon and go inside before the storm arrived.

Adrian crouched behind some bushes along with Bridget. When she had collected enough rocks, she gave him a kiss and hurried to the other side of the tree, staying in the shadows. Adrian waited for her to shoot the first rock before he made his move.

He noticed when a rock hit his cousin's hooded head. Walden yelped and rubbed the spot where the rock had hit. It didn't take very long for him to continue striking the axe against the branch. Seconds later, another rock hit him. This time, it was on his shoulder. The axe slipped from Walden's hands, but he quickly stopped it from falling to the ground.

Walden crouched on the branch, unmoving. Adrian could tell his cousin was scoping out the yard because of the way the hood turned from right to left, but knew he wouldn't see anything due to the many shadows. Adrian had never given his cousin credit for having a lick of sense, mainly because the man had always been coddled by *Mother Dearest*. So, was this plan to kill Collin and Adrian for a title really Walden's idea? Did the grown man with a childlike mind really have the smarts to act out like this? Or had being mentally challenged been a cover for his vindictive ways all along?

Suddenly, another rock struck the fool in the tree, and he cried out. This time, the axe fell from his hands and landed on the ground. The grumblings coming from Adrian's cousin were clearly heard as he hurried to climb down the many branches.

Another rock was shot at Walden, and the *kerthunk* against the man's noggin was louder than before.

"Ouch!" He rubbed his head again.

Smiling, Adrian shook his head, hardly believing how good Bridget was at using the slingshot. He loved her playfulness. Most women in society would have scoffed at the mere idea of using a slingshot. Then again, most women were not as clever as his Bridget.

Just as Walden reached the spot where the ladder leaned against the tree, the next rock hit the ladder, knocking it over. His loud, surprised gasp ripped through the air.

"What—who is out there?" Walden stammered.

Another rock zipped through the air and hit the man's chest, and he released a small cry as he rubbed at the targeted area. He positioned himself in the tree so he could slide down the trunk, but another rock sailed through the night air and slammed right into his buttocks. Walden screamed like a little girl and fell out of the tree. He scrambled to his feet, but another rock hit his leg, and he crumpled to the ground.

Adrian hurried out of his hiding place and stopped right in front of his cousin. Folding his arms across his chest, he glared at the foolish man.

When Walden looked up, a gust of wind blew off his hood. He stared up with wide, frightened eyes.

Adrian shook his head. "I should have known it was you."

"I… I don't know what you are referring to, milord."

Adrian rolled his eyes. "I know you have always been dense, but I thought you would know by now when to accept failure."

He kicked Walden's black boot. "Admit to me now that you are responsible for all the accidents that have been happening recently."

"Wh-what accidents?"

Adrian blew out a frustrated breath. "Collin's saddle girth being cut, and then his being shot at. And let's not forget when the railing on the stairs was broken and a plant fell off the banister and nearly landed on me."

Walden shook his head quickly. "I didn't do that." Another rock sailed through the air and hit Walden's arm. He cried out and rubbed the spot, swinging his head back and forth as he searched through the shadows for the person attacking him. "Who is doing this to me?"

Adrian crouched to his cousin's level. "I'll make a deal with you. If you tell my father everything you've been doing, I'll make the rocks stop striking you."

"N-no. I… didn't do it."

Adrian shrugged and stood. Seconds later, another rock slammed into his cousin's jaw. Walden sobbed as his fingers flew to the reddened spot. A drop of blood appeared on his chin.

"All you have to do is tell me," Adrian continued, "and I'll stop the rocks from hitting you."

Tears filled Walden's eyes. "I didn't want to do this." His voice cracked. "This was my mother's idea, not mine."

Shock was like a bolt of lightning zipping through Adrian, and he stumbled backward. "*Aunt Beatrice*? The woman who has pretended to be my mother since my own parent died? Impossible."

Walden nodded vigorously. "Yes. My mother wanted Collin's title to go to me."

Anger filled Adrian, and he wanted to shake some sense into his aunt. Betrayal from her actions left a bitter taste in his mouth and a painful knot in his gut. But that explained why she had shown up to the ball without an invitation, and why she insisted on staying to oversee the living arrangements, even though he'd tried to convince her she wasn't needed here.

He reached out and helped his cousin stand. "I'll go with you into the manor, and I expect you to tell my father and everyone in that room what you and your mother have done."

Tears fell down Walden's red cheeks in buckets now. "I'm sorry, Lord William. I… I really didn't want the title, but Mother forced me to do it."

"Come on," Adrian snapped. "You can tell that to the others. They wouldn't believe me if I tried explaining this. In fact, I'm having a difficult time believing this is all real."

He glanced over his shoulder toward where Bridget had been, and he motioned with his hand for her come over. "We are done, my love. It's getting too chilly to be out here now."

She hurried next to him, and he wrapped an arm around her shoulders as they walked toward the house.

Walden dragged his feet as he moved toward the manor. Adrian almost felt sorry for his cousin. However, he would *not* feel sorry for Aunt Beatrice. Hopefully, his father punished her for her crimes.

"Are you going to be all right?" Bridget asked.

"Eventually I will. It's just hard to believe a woman who has been like a second mother to us would do such a thing."

"I'm sorry you had to go through that." She slid her arms around his waist as they walked into the house.

The closer they walked toward the sitting room, the more the silence in the sitting room bothered him. Had Walden taken the coward's way out?

Anger quickened Adrian's gait until he stopped at the doorway. Walden stood in the room, shifting from one foot to the other, as he wrung his hands against his chest. Everyone's attention was on the foolish man who didn't know how to say no to his mother.

"What is it, boy?" Adrian's father asked, his voice filled with impatience.

"I… I…"

Walden glanced over his shoulder toward Adrian, who glared. Indeed, if the foolish man didn't confess now, Adrian would beat it out of him.

"Speak up, Walden," Aunt Beatrice said. "We don't have all evening to watch you stammer. You have interrupted our conversation, so if you don't have anything to say, then leave."

Walden's shoulders straightened as he pierced his mother with a scowl. "You have always talked down to me as if I'm stupid. But I'm not. If I'm anything, I'm obedient, and... I have had enough of your abuse."

"Abuse?" Aunt Beatrice's voice lifted in irritation. "Walden, what has come over you to talk such nonsense?"

"My lord," Walden continued, looking at Adrian's father. "I have something to tell you and Lord Hanover." He inhaled deeply and licked his swollen lips. "Mother wants me to have Collin's title, and she forced me to create accidents around the manor in order to harm—or kill—my cousins."

"*What?*" Adrian's father jumped to his feet. His eyes widened in shock, but seconds later, he marched toward his sister, grasped her arm, and yanked her out of the chair. "I had a feeling you were behind this. You were always jealous of my sons, but I never thought you would be insane enough to try to kill your own flesh and blood."

"No," Aunt Beatrice gasped. "Walden is lying. He's not right in the head. Never has been, in fact."

Walden shook his head and glared at his mother. "I will never let you control my life again, witch."

"Gilbert?" Adrian's father called. Seconds later, the butler hurried into the room.

"Yes, my lord."

"Fetch the constable, posthaste. I want these two arrested." He motioned toward his sister and Walden. "And they are never to enter any of my estates again. They are both dead to me."

"Father," Adrian said quickly, moving to his father. "I believe Walden. Knowing how controlling Aunt Beatrice is, we know

now what she is capable of. None of this was Walden's fault. His only crime was going along with what his mother told him to do."

Adrian's father's nostrils flared. The man's face was still red, and his chest rose and fell quickly from his fast breaths. "Fine, but I never want to see my sister again."

Collin stomped to the older woman and snatched her wrist. The look he gave her was murderous. "You will never again get the chance to harm me or my family. I *will* make certain you are thrown in the gaol and the keeper throws away the key to your cell."

The older woman scowled at Adrian as Collin pulled her out of the room. Adrian couldn't hide the hurt that he felt, and he hoped guilt would eventually consume her and she would have to live with her mistakes for the rest of her life.

He took Bridget's hand, lifted it to his mouth, and brushed a kiss across her knuckles. "You are absolutely amazing, my love."

She smiled. "Why do you say that?"

"For two reasons, actually. First, because it was your idea how to get Walden to confess, and secondly, because I have never seen a woman use a slingshot so effectively and effortlessly."

She chuckled. "You should watch my younger sisters sometime. I'm just an amateur compared to them."

He laughed. "What am I marrying into?" he said jokingly.

She waggled her brows. "That, my dear Adrian, is just a hint of the adventures awaiting you after we are wed."

His grin widened. "I cannot wait. Life with you will be a dream come true."

Epilogue

BRIDGET COULDN'T STOP staring at Adrian. He made such a handsome husband. Of course, it was the love shining in his perfect eyes that caused her heartbeat to flip-flop with happiness. And now they were married, she looked forward to spending a lifetime with him and having his children.

Their wedding had been a big event—not only in their small village but in the neighboring townships—and so many guests attended. The manor was decorated both inside and outside, but the weather was so lovely that she and Adrian had spent most of their time outside. She was introduced to many people and worried she would forget them by the next day.

During a break in the evening when nobody accosted them, Adrian walked her toward the stream that flowed through the yard and to the small bridge over it. Not much was said, and she was certain her husband wanted a private moment just as she did.

Adrian led her to the top of the bridge and stopped on the gentle arch of the wooden structure. Smiling down at her, he stroked her cheek.

"Do you know how happy you have made me?"

"If you are as happy as I am at this very moment, I think I know how you feel. If everyone could feel this way, the world would be a much better place."

"I agree, my love." He pulled her closer, and she pressed the side of her face against his chest. "Has your sister said anything to you about Collin proposing?"

"Not one word." She frowned. "I don't dare say anything to her in case your brother has changed his mind about Lady Kentwood."

"Yes, I, too, don't dare mention anything to Collin. I don't want him to think I'm pushing him."

"He seems quite content lately. Perhaps he is not thinking of that other woman any longer."

"We can only hope."

Across the lawn, an attractive man and woman strolled their way. The lovely woman with blonde hair had her arm hooked around the elbow of the tall man with dark brown hair. The man smiled widely and waved.

"Come, my love," Adrian said, "and let me introduce you to my favorite cousin."

They walked off the bridge and toward the other couple. When they reached them, both the man and woman gave Adrian a hearty hug. Adrian stepped back and slid his arm around Bridget's waist.

"My love, let me introduce you to Lord Trey Worthington, and his lovely wife, Lady Judith Worthington." He looked at his cousin. "And this is Lady Bridget Worthington."

Bridget smiled and curtsied. She loved being called *Lady* Worthington.

"We just heard about your brother's new title." Trey grinned. "Marquess of Kentwood, eh?"

Adrian nodded. "Indeed. It's rather remarkable, is it not?"

"Although it is remarkable," Judith added, "I'm sorry to hear about Lloyd's death."

"Did you know him?" Adrian asked.

"Sadly, no." Judith frowned. "Only what my husband said about him."

"Well, do not waste your sympathy on that man. He was a rotten gambler. He made more enemies than friends."

Suddenly, the crowd in the yard quieted, but one lone voice ripped through the air, disturbing the silence. All heads swung toward the woman wearing a silver and blue gown cut in a fashion Bridget had never seen before—the gown's waist being lower than was currently fashionable. The woman's blonde hair was fixed in an elegant twist on top of her head, and a few tendrils hung by her ears.

She stood in front of Collin, scowling. The surprised look on his face made Bridget wonder if he knew her. The woman was extremely irate, evidenced by her loud voice and the way she flung her arms in wild gestures.

"You ruined my family because of your deceitful actions," the lady shouted. "And you ruined... *my* life!"

Bridget was embarrassed, not only for the outraged woman with so many spectators around, but also for Collin, who had obviously been very reckless in his past.

"Cassandra—"

"I'm *Lady* Kentwood to you!"

Trey sucked in a loud breath. "Oh my... The rumors are true."

Adrian groaned and rubbed his forehead. "Yes, they are."

Bridget frowned. Gossip would spread like wildfire now. This was not good. And where was her sister? Bridget prayed Priscilla wasn't hearing any of this, but the chances were against her. Poor Priscilla's heart would be shattered.

Finally, Collin straightened his shoulders and moved closer to the woman. He nodded toward the manor. "I think that we should take this conversation somewhere that is more private."

"*Private?*" she shrieked. "Why? So you can ruin my reputation even more?"

"Lady Kentwood." Collin's expression hardened. "I really must insist."

"You can insist all you like for the good it will do," the lady snapped, "but I will never willingly go into a private room with you ever again."

Adrian released another groan, and this time, Bridget joined him. Collin must be humiliated, and to be honest, she was getting a little upset that the woman showed no scruples or decorum. After all, she was making her already *ruined* reputation worse by airing her grievances in public—and at a wedding party, no less.

"Cousin?" Adrian grumbled.

Trey looked at him. "Yes?"

"Would you like to help me break up this scene and escort the lady off our property?"

"Gladly."

As the two men marched toward Collin, Bridget wrung her hands at her waist and searched for Priscilla. Her sister was probably devastated and would need comforting. Bridget spotted her standing with Felicia and Jannette. Both the younger sisters had their arms protectively around a white-faced Priscilla. Bridget's chest tightened as she felt the humiliation her sister was experiencing now.

It didn't take long before Adrian and Trey were able to escort Lady Kentwood toward her waiting coach, but as soon as the woman climbed inside and the driver pulled away, Collin snapped out of his stupor and ran toward the vehicle. Adrian tried to stop him, but he pushed his brother away, mounted a horse, and rode after the coach.

Within moments, the crowd began talking in low voices, which gradually grew louder. Felicia and Jannette took Priscilla inside the manor.

Bridget hurried toward them, but Adrian stopped her and took her in his arms.

"I'm so sorry this happened at our wedding," he whispered in her ear.

Nodding, she looked into his eyes. "My poor sister."

"Yes. I'm sure this has broken her heart."

He kissed Bridget's forehead. "We shall help her get through this. In fact..." He smiled. "I have a few friends who are in need of a good wife to straighten them out."

Bridget gasped, but then a chuckle bubbled up from her

throat. "You cannot be serious."

"But I am."

"Are your friends anything like you?"

He grimaced. "Probably a little worse."

"Oh, heavens. Well, I'm sure Felicia and Jannette might find their bold personalities compatible, but sweet Priscilla needs someone gentler and less roguish in the ways of the world."

"I have an idea." He cuddled her closer. "Let's make it our quest to help your sisters find good husbands. I'll sponsor their Seasons, as well."

Sighing, Bridget placed her hands on her husband's strong chest as she gazed into his dreamy eyes. "I'm so very glad I married a man with a heart of gold, and every day I'm with you, I get to see your kindness in action." She toyed with his cravat. "I believe between the two of us, we can find husbands for my sisters. And maybe"—she arched an eyebrow—"find a good wife for your brother."

Adrian threw back his head and laughed. "I fear, my lovely wife, that my brother will be a bigger challenge than we are prepared for."

"I'm ready to tackle it. Aren't you?"

He cupped her face. "With you, I will be able to handle anything life throws at me."

As he kissed her, it didn't surprise her that they were kissing in public and might create a scene, but it did surprise her that her husband was up for the challenge of matchmaking. It thrilled her, because now she knew how much he loved her… Enough to do *anything*.

THE END

Other published stories by Marie Higgins
www.authormariehiggins.com/books

Join my newsletter and start your reading collection.
www.authormariehiggins.com/newsletter

About the Author

Marie Higgins is an award-winning, best-selling author of clean romance novels that melt your heart and have you falling in love over and over again. Since 2010, she's published over 100 heartwarming, on-the-edge-of-your-seat romances. She has broadened her readership by writing mystery/suspense, humor, time travel, and paranormal, along with her love for historical romances. Her readers have dubbed her "Queen of Tease" because of all her twists and unexpected endings.

Website – www.authormariehiggins.com
Facebook – facebook.com/marie.higgins.7543
TikTok – tiktok.com/@author.mariehiggins
Instagram – instagram.com/author.mariehiggins
Bookbub – bookbub.com/authors/marie-higgins

www.ingramcontent.com/pod-product-compliance
Lightning Source LLC
Chambersburg PA
CBHW070356200726
48294CB00003B/944

* 9 7 8 1 9 6 1 2 7 5 6 0 7 *